T0367943

Pulse
Of
Desire

Pulse
Of
Desire

Julianna Pinkhasova

Archway Publishing books may be ordered through booksellers or by contacting:

Archway Publishing
1663 Liberty Drive
Bloomington, IN 47403
www.archwaypublishing.com
844-669-3957

ISBN: 978-1-6657-6185-7 (sc)
ISBN: 978-1-6657-6187-1 (hc)
ISBN: 978-1-6657-6186-4 (e)

Library of Congress Control Number: 2024912563

Print information available on the last page.

Archway Publishing rev. date: 07/23/2024

———

For all who love the medical field.

Violet

"ONE ... TWO ... THREE." I GRUNT, DROPPING THE SIX-POUND weights to the ground. Yeah, I definitely need to take a moment to catch my breath. I place my hands on my hips and tilt my head back, taking a deep breath. They are only six-pound weights. How am I struggling this much? I just started my gym membership an hour ago, and clearly, there's a lot of work to do. Plus, working on my body is a great way to start my summer vacation before starting my freshman year of college. The stench of sweat abruptly hits my nose. Really? I'm sweating already? I bend over, reaching my toes, and then stretch my arm across my body. Then I do the same with my other arm.

I know I should be increasing my calorie intake since being ninety pounds at twenty years old isn't ideal, but working out can be helpful too. Clearly, it's been a struggle, and it hasn't even been two hours of working out, which was the goal. For years, I couldn't understand what was wrong with me. Why haven't I been gaining weight like a normal person? Then again, I would've had my question answered if I would be more compliant at doctor visits. Even the hospital couldn't figure out why I'm like this, but that was years ago. Just remembering the hospital gives me goosebumps all over my body, even though I am sweating right now.

I've had this gaining-weight problem ever since fifth grade, and I have no clue why. I'm hoping that building muscle can make some sort of difference, so here I am, attempting to work out.

In about two months, I'll be a student at Queens College, which is exciting, but I still haven't decided what I want to major in. If there's something I'm more than sure about it's that there is no way I'll go into anything related to medicine. Not sure why exactly, but ever since I was ten years old, I've had an irrational fear of doctors and medical tests. The memory of the medical office makes me squirm, and I have a feeling my pediatrician is still traumatized by me.

My phone vibrates with some number calling me that I don't recognize. It's probably the doctor's office calling to confirm my appointment for today. I roll my eyes and decline the call.

Every doctor's visit for the past ten years has been absolute hell for my mom. I don't blame her for lashing out at the end of every physical. I admit that I was always immoderately difficult. It's the fear that gets in the way of all the medical stuff. I wish I knew where the fear emerged from and how.

Which reminds me ... I'm supposed to go to my doctor's appointment later at 6:00 p.m., hence the call I just got. I chuckle at the slim possibility of me going to my appointment. No way in hell will I go through that torture again. Mom is the one who scheduled that appointment for me, since she knows I won't schedule it myself, and I haven't gotten a checkup in over a year. She's concerned, and I *should* be too. It's about time ... I guess. Except Mom doesn't have to know that I'm ditching my dreadful six o'clock appointment. I don't feel all that amused by the expectation that I'll faint at the hands of the doctor who's taking my blood. I jog in place so that I'm not wasting a single minute of my gym subscription. I want to make the most out of it.

It's been five minutes. I think I'll give the weights another go. I try squatting and lifting the weights at the same time to make more of a difference.

Here we go again. Is he still staring at me? I quickly look to my side and then look away. Yep, he's still at it.

That same guy with crazy-toned abs and a hot face has been staring at me with a grin this entire time. I should be flattered, really, but I'm mostly creeped out. Like, if there's something he wants to tell me, why doesn't he just get it over with and say it?

I stop watching him from the corner of my eye and finally do a full-body turn to face him eye to eye.

"Can I help you?" I ask in hopes he'll mind his own business.

He drops his serious expression and smiles. "Nah, but I'm gathering that you could use some help."

I cock my head to the side and scrunch up my face as though I'm confused. "Excuse me?"

"Oh, I didn't mean to come off rude, but I was conflicted whether or not to approach and show you an easier strategy for lifting weights since you seem to be struggling."

"Struggling, huh? What are you? Some kind of expert?"

"I wouldn't call it being an expert … more of an enthusiast of working out, and I don't enjoy watching anyone struggling."

Still, that's none of his business.

"So, you're finding this as an opportunity to make fun of me?" I joke.

He laughs. "Yeah, well, maybe just a little. Um, I've never seen you here before. Did you just start your membership?"

He's hitting on me. I'm 100 percent sure.

"Yeah, I just started an hour ago. You?"

"I've been going to this gym for a few years. I never miss a single weekend." He puts his weight down and comes closer. "I'm Elliot by the way."

My cheeks flush. He looks so much more flattering close up. My jaw feels weak.

Elliot is such a cute name. I remember my childhood crush had that name. Unfortunately, my crush Elliot was related to an annoying kid named Adam. I don't remember why I was so afraid of him, but I think it was because he was always obsessively pursuing me, and according to my friend Karen from back then, he would touch me and force me to go through with something I hated. I have no memory of Adam doing anything out of the ordinary to me. Karen never specified what she meant by him forcing me to go through something. She could've been lying about it, but why would she? Unless Adam told her to, but there's no proof of that. Eh, who cares. I'm over all that by now. It was all just childhood drama.

"I'm Violet."

"Hold on … You're Violet," he repeats, surprised.

I pause and stare at him, confused.

"Wow … I was wondering why you looked so familiar," Elliot says in astonishment.

"What are you talking about? Do we know each other?"

"Sixth grade, remember? We were both in Ms. Macooley's homeroom class."

Holy crap.

"No way! Wait, that's crazy … Elliot? Whoa, um … you changed a lot."

He laughs. "Yeah, I finally got rid of that lame haircut."

"Oh, c'mon, don't say that. I loved your haircut. It was really cute."

I mean it. His brunette hair perfectly complimented his face, and it still does. His round, hazel eyes are what stand out the most. They're just perfect.

"Time flies, huh?" He sighs.

I never got to admit to Elliot that I liked him, but we were only kids, so what's the harm in bringing it up now?

"You know what's funny? I actually had a crush on you back in sixth grade," I say in a playful tone.

"Seriously? That's so cute! I liked you too … just never had the courage to say anything at the time."

We both laugh.

"Good times."

His vibrating phone interrupts the moment. Elliot's face looks alarmed at the sight of his phone screen. He looks out past the glass doors as though he's looking for something … or someone.

"Ah, shoot. I've gotta run."

I clear my throat and straighten up.

"Of course. It was nice seeing you again, Elliot."

"You too!"

He nearly runs out of the gym but stops midway and turns back, approaching me.

"Before I go, how about we exchange numbers—you know, so maybe you and I can go out sometime?"

I freeze. That was the last thing I expected he would say, but I'm not complaining.

"Sure! Here, I'll put my number into your phone."

He enters his passcode, and I take his phone. Once my contact is saved, I hand the phone back.

"I'll text you later!" he says on his way out, smiling widely.

"Sounds great. See you!" I respond as I watch him leave.

Well, that went pretty well. Elliot was cute back then, but

now that he's gotten a glow up, he's just perfect. Even if we were to date, I can't expect anything yet. We were only kids back then, and who knows how he turned out to be. I still need to get to know him, and holy hell, there's so much I want to know, like what he's majoring in and what college he's in. The basics, of course.

I'm kind of hungry, so I'll stop working out for today. I put the weights back and go to the changing room to get back into my casual clothing. One hour of working out is a good start … I think.

Suddenly, I feel my phone vibrating in my back pocket. Interesting. It's a message from an unsaved number.

> Unsaved number: Hey, it's Elliot. I just cleared my schedule for this evening. Can I pick you up at seven?

That was fast. My heart is racing out of my chest. Holy crap. Should I say yes? I mean, this would be a great excuse for missing my appointment since I didn't have a ready excuse before, and he's really attractive.

> Me: Hey, I'll save your contact. ;) Sure! Where are we going?

I press send. Elliot's message pops up almost immediately.

> Elliot: A really cool restaurant. I think you'll love it. ;)

> Me: Super! I'll send you my address.

I send him my address shortly after sending that message. Oh my gosh. Is this really happening? I haven't gone on a date since I was eighteen years old. It was a complete failure, since the guy went on while telling his sob stories about all his exes. It was a huge red flag, and it was definitely my last time talking to him. That was my first date, which makes this one my second. I get asked out on dates a crazy ton, but I never seem to let my guard down and just go. All the guys who've asked me out on dates were just not my cup of tea. Elliot is an exception though. We liked each other as kids, and yeah, I know that doesn't mean anything, but I still want to give him a chance. I have this strange, gut feeling that something big might just happen tonight. I hope that's a good thing. The only downside of dating Elliot is his older brother Adam, whom I was intimidated by in fifth grade. Who knows … maybe Adam has changed since we were kids and he doesn't have that fear inducing effect on me, but I can't be 100 percent sure of that yet. I remember I would tremble around Adam, and he was always staring at me. I also vaguely remember him cackling. Not sure what that was all about. I haven't seen Adam in years, and a part of me wants it to stay that way. If anything, I'll ask Elliot about his brother and see what's new with him. The worst that could happen is Adam getting in between Elliot and me. That's only if Adam is still not over me, which would be concerning. It's been ten years, so he probably forgot about me. I hope so.

2

Violet

I'VE BEEN WATCHING THE TIME LIKE A HAWK THE CLOSER IT ticks to 7:00 p.m. I was all dressed up and ready about an hour ago, and at any given moment, Elliot should be here to pick me up for our date. I put on a casual fit: a red top, ripped jeans, and one-inch black heels. My phone buzzes with a message from Elliot.

> Elliot: I just pulled up. My car is in front of your
> house.

I nearly trip over my feet out of excitement as I get into Elliot's black Mercedes.

"Whoa, neat ride!"

He smiles at my comment. "Thanks, it's my brother's. He let me borrow it for our date."

"You don't have your own car?" I ask.

He shakes his head. "Adam and I are sharing this car until mine is finished getting repaired. It's a long story."

I catch sight of Elliot's navigation that shows that our

destination is five minutes away. Elliot turns up the radio, which is playing, "Don't Stop Believin'."

It's not something I typically listen to, but I won't judge him.

"Does Adam know you're taking me on a date tonight?"

Elliot acts like he doesn't hear me and continues vibing to the music.

"Does he?" I ask again to push him to answer.

"Huh? Oh, you mean my brother Adam? Yeah, I told him."

Elliot's responses are vague. Is there a good reason as to why? I stare at him politely as though I'm waiting for him to continue talking. He notices I'm staring and freezes.

"Why do you ask?" He sounds skeptical.

"No good reason. Just that it's been a while and I haven't heard from him since we were kids."

He looks relieved at my response.

"Oh. Yeah, Adam is doing just fine. He's gotten into the same college as me actually."

"Sounds great! What college?"

"Queens College."

My jaw drops. "No way! I go to that college too. What are you both majoring in?"

Elliot abruptly turns his head to look at me, alerted like I've said something that shocked him. He hesitates and laughs nervously.

"Well, we're both going into the medical field to become primary-care physicians. I wanna be a pediatrician though."

It looks like Elliot's face paled from just answering my question. I feel the goosebumps growing back all over my arms. It's almost like Elliot knew I'd get uncomfortable and turned off by him mentioning the medical field, because of how afraid he seemed about my response. I won't make it seem like I'm affected though. The last thing I need is to scare off my date before we even get to our destination.

He looks at my arms, which are covered in goosebumps.

"Are you cold?"

"No, no, I'm OK. The goosebumps show when I'm nervous," I lie.

He smiles generously. "You're nervous? How come?"

I exhale. "It's just I haven't been on a date in a long time, so it feels like a first for me."

"Aww, don't worry. I don't bite on first dates."

What a peculiar way of responding. He looks at me as though surprised I'm not treating what he said as a joke.

"I don't bite on dates in general," he adds, giggling.

He's weird for saying that. "I didn't assume you did." I try smiling to mimic his current energy, even though what he said was so random.

He pulls over suddenly. "We're here."

"What is this place?" I ask as I step out of the car.

"It's a buffet. I figured you may like selecting the food on your own instead of waiting for a waiter."

Holy crap, he is fancy.

"Whoa, Elliot. For a first date, this seems stupendous." My eyes light up. I love buffets. I get resort vibes from them.

"I knew you'd love it!"

"I didn't say I love it yet. I've still gotta try the food."

"Sassy Miss Violet." He beams.

"So far, A+ for presentation," I say gleefully.

He winks at me. We each grab a plate on the buffet stand. We take some salads from the front of the stand before going to the next section. This is the perfect opportunity to start talking to get to know one another.

"I told you what I'm majoring in. What about you?" he asks as he scoops rice onto his plate.

"Actually, I don't really know yet."

"Well, do you have any ideas?"

"All I know is there's no way I'll go anywhere in the medical field." I squirm at the memory of my blood flowing out of my vein into a blood collection tube.

Elliot pauses and looks at me amusedly.

"Why is that, I wonder? Is it because of the long number of years to become a doctor?"

I exhale quickly. "Not at all. I don't mind learning longer. I love school. It's just the blood work, needles, doctors being touchy, and a whole lot of other crap that I really can't tolerate."

Oh my gosh ... that was me opening up, and it happened so fast. I should've waited a while longer. Elliot looks more amused than ever. His eyes widen curiously, like he's longing to know more.

"Hmm. A few bad experiences made you hate doctors, huh?"

"More like every experience. I was actually supposed to be at my appointment at 6:00 p.m. today, but I ditched."

I face him. He looks annoyed. Disrespected almost.

"You ditched?"

"Yeah ... I prefer to avoid that kind of torture as much as humanly possible."

He dramatically blinks hard at me. "Torture? ... I don't suppose I can change your mind about doctors. Can I?"

"Nope. I'm afraid nothing can—and I don't want to." We turn to the other side of the buffet stand. "Why do you want to be a pediatrician?"

He stops to explain. "The human body is like a whole other

world to explore. It interests me. That and I adore younger kids."

"Aww, that's sweet that you like kids. Do you have any little siblings?"

"Well, not little, but I have two brothers. One, as you know, is Adam, who's a year older than me, and my younger brother is Nathan. He's two years younger than me."

"Let me guess, Nathan is a medical enthusiast as well?"

He laughs. "Hey, how'd you know?" he asks sarcastically.

"But yeah, we are all into medical stuff. I won't go in depth about it since it's only our first date, so I'll save that for another day."

We take our food-piled plates to the nearest table and take a seat.

"The food here is amazing! I love it!"

He smiles proudly. "There you go! See? It's like I know you so well already."

I smile back at him. "Or you know all of the coolest places to dine at."

"This is nothing compared to other places I know. You'll see. Next time, I'll take you there."

Holy hell, I am in the deepest depths of paradise.

"Oh, so there is a next time with you?"

"Of course! I love talking to you. That and you are really enticing."

My cheeks flush. He's such a sweetheart.

We spent the rest of our ten minutes only eating, since the mariachi band rudely played insanely loud music over our date. We just shrugged and laughed most of the time. Now, I'm certain that there has to be a next date. There is still so much to learn from Elliot. I got really lucky for joining the gym when I did; otherwise, I wouldn't be sitting here vibing with the coolest guy ever. Never mind that he's a medical enthusiast. That shouldn't bother me as long as he isn't the one giving me physicals. As Elliot is paying our dinner bill, I notice an interesting device attached to his necklace. It almost looks like a microphone.

"What's that around your neck?" I ask out of curiosity.

He looks and averts his eyes. "A necklace that Adam got me."

The only time that Elliot acts strangely suspicious is when I bring up Adam. Weird.

"Ready to go?" he asks as he stands up with his bag.

"Yep, let's go."

We leave and hop into his car immediately since it's starting to drizzle rain outside.

"You know, my house is just a block away and it looks like there will be a storm according to the weather app. You wanna come in until it stops raining?" he asks convincingly.

"Gee, thanks, but I think I better get home now. It's getting kinda late."

"Oh c'mon. I insist."

I hesitate since I'm feeling tired from all the food that we just ate. "Yeah, but my house is like five minutes away."

He looks at me with puppy-dog eyes to jokingly convince me. I laugh. "Uh, fine. I'll go with you, but only for a little. It's almost 9:00 p.m."

We make a few turns until we finally reach Elliot's house. He pulls up into his driveway, and we leave his car.

"Come on in. Make yourself at home," Elliot gestures into his house.

Whoa ...! His house is huge inside. I mean, the exterior seems small, but I can't say the same about the interior.

Sudden dread surges through me as a familiar, smug face peeks out from behind a door. Is that ... Adam?

My legs stiffen as he approaches me. Crazy how he still has this intimidating effect on me even ten years later. I still don't get why I get uncomfortable in his presence.

Before anyone gets the chance to break the silence, my phone rings. Adam looks alarmed at this sudden interference, and he exchanges concerned glances with Elliot.

I eye my phone. "Um ... hold on, I've gotta take this. It's my mom."

Elliot steps back. "Sure, take your time."

"Hey, mom, What's up?"

"Violet, we've been waiting on you for over an hour. Where are you?"

Crap. I completely forgot about the guests that are coming over today. I was supposed to be helping mom prepare dinner after my doctor's appointment, but honestly, I'm not complaining that I missed out on that. I would much rather be here vibing with Elliot. I briefly smile at him and gesture that everything is all right, and he gives me a thumbs up.

"Oh yeah, the guests! I'll be right over. I just finished my date because I got an email that my doctor's appointment was transferred to another day."

"Okay honey, that's fine. Ooh, a date? Who's the lucky guy?" my mom asks with inflection.

My cheeks flush. "I'll tell you all about it when I get home. He's in the same room as me."

"Oh, sorry. OK, come quick!"

The call ends, and I turn back to face the brothers.

"I've gotta go. My family is waiting on me."

"Don't worry, you don't have to explain yourself. Family time is important," Elliot replies.

I nod. "Until next time?"

Adam is staring at me with hostility. He doesn't move a muscle or blink while he watches me interact with his brother.

"Of course! Let me drive you back home."

I hesitate. I don't want to be a burden. Also, I hate to make it seem like I'm crushing hard on Elliot in front of Adam.

"It's fine, the walk home isn't too far."

Adam elbows Elliot as he stares at me shamelessly.

"She's right, Elliot. The way back home isn't far. Let her go," Adam says with a hint of annoyance in his voice.

Elliot makes a face like he just realized what Adam is getting at. I'm still super confused. "All right, well, get home safe." Elliot smiles, and I leave the house still being followed out by Adam's stare.

There's something really odd about Adam, but I can't quite put my finger on it. The moment I said I had to leave, Adam made it seem as though I was an inconvenience to them. I'm not that surprised … mostly puzzled. I just know that I'll be fantasizing Elliot and I together my entire walk home.

3

Adam

I STARE AT ELLIOT, HIS DEFEATED DEMEANOR ECHOING MY frustration. I swear I've trained Elliot to be better than this. What the hell is wrong with him? After years of trying … this could've been the beginning of mine and Violet's destiny together—the type of destiny that involves the best scientific explorations in the human body.

"Elliot, I thought I taught you better! You had one job, and you screwed up our best shot."

Elliot puts his arms over his head. "OK, look. None of this is my fault! I got her this far. Can't you at least give me credit for that?" he pleads, his voice tinged with desperation.

I roll my eyes at his pathetic response.

"Did you not think to take her phone? Someone could easily track her while it's turned on."

Elliot's quick exhale filled the tense silence.

"Would you calm down? Our next date will be right around the corner. I assure you that she'll be ours before you know it."

As I listen to his words, a surge of determination courses through me. He's right. There's still time. If it wasn't for that shot that I gave Violet back in fifth grade, she would remember my intentions. There really wasn't anything in the shot other than a weak tranquilizer that I stole from my aunt's medical practice. Instead, I caused a placebo effect with the tranquilizer to the effect that if Violet got that shot, she wouldn't remember anything I did to her. I'm honestly very surprised that it even worked. It was a risky move but totally worth it in the end. I know that once I'm a real doctor, I can get patients at any time, but out of all of them, my eyes are on Violet. I'm still working on her medical case, and I still have questions that haven't been answered. I've never met anyone with an odd case like hers.

Beyond my obsession with Violet is my passion for the medical field. I can't separate the two—they have always been intertwined in my mind. Since so long ago, Violet's condition has fascinated me, driving me to research tirelessly in hopes of finding a solution. I couldn't stand by and watch her struggle, not when I knew I had the knowledge to help her. What would I get out of curing my dearest Violet? Simple. I would have a person to study and practice medicine on. I need someone to help me with my medical studies by playing the role of my guinea pig, and Violet is the perfect match for this role. I'd say she's the luckiest girl in the world with someone like me wanting to heal her in *our* best interests.

Based on her physical profile, she's really underweight, which I find very concerning and not exactly a characteristic of someone I would want to marry. I mean, I'm not some superficial jerk, but I want someone who's healthy, and seeing Violet like that just breaks my heart.

I remember in the beginning of fifth grade, she used to eat like a champ during lunch, always asking for seconds from the lunch ladies like she was starving. I don't know where all that food went in her body, but clearly, none of it gave her the proper nourishment that she needs. It's like her body was just refusing to cooperate, no matter how much she ate.

Toward the end of the fifth grade, though, something changed. She barely ate lunch—almost like she'd given up on it. I can't blame her ... she must have thought that it was pointless to keep trying to gain weight if nothing seemed to work. I'd always kept watch over her, until one day I decided to take matters into my own hands. It's about time that I step in and become the hero she deserves in her life.

I was determined to conduct physical examinations on her. I couldn't stand watching the poor girl struggle so much. I remember it hurt so much to watch her during lunch sometimes. I felt really bad, and it pissed me off how nobody else cared like I did. It was probably because all the rest of the idiots in that class were plump enough to fill the largest clothing. Then again, I guess not everyone sees things the way I do.

Not only that, but I genuinely felt bad because I, myself, was very underweight in the most vile way possible. No doctor could ever figure out what was wrong with me, but when I got a little older, I conducted tests on myself. I worked myself until I developed and caught up to the weight that I should have been for my age. As it turns out, I had many nutrient deficiencies, which stunted my development. Crazy, right?

I'm not sure how doctors never caught that, but it made me think that they didn't care. I'm sure none of them ever did; otherwise, I would've been in better condition way earlier.

Now, it is my job to heal Violet. Most of the pathetic doctors out there don't care about the patient and are gobbling up as much money as they can get their hands on. Me, on the other hand? I'm the complete opposite. I actually care, and I may be the only person who can fix Violet.

Every night, I did plenty of research on metabolisms and the key components necessary to maintain a healthy body weight, as well as deep research on biology itself. Violet is the whole reason I want to become a doctor in the first place. If it wasn't for me pitying her in the fifth grade, none of this would've come into play. I did enough research as a kid to have passed an entire semester of college biology.

I remember my friends thought I was crazy for even considering going through with examining Violet, but luckily, I was able to blackmail many of them into doing my bidding. A surge of pleasure flows through me as I remember my friends and classmates holding down Violet in the empty classroom while I gave her physicals. I miss those moments dearly. What sucked was when I no longer had classes with Violet to continue my research on her. To this day, she struggles with her unhealthy weight, and it seems rather dangerous. Is nobody taking care of her? I mean, this is serious ... she can't be living like this. It hurts me to know she still has this physical condition and that I am powerless to help her—for now, at least.

At first, I assumed that her condition was genetic, but after seeing her parents at dismissal all those years ago, it seemed like they struggled losing weight rather than gaining. An eating disorder was my next guess, but I needed more medical evidence to back that up. So far, I've got nothing, but it's not my fault! It was hard enough giving her check-ups secretly in school while she would try to escape.

To an average person, my obsession with Violet's well-being might seem all for nothing, but that's because nobody understands that I want to spend the rest of my life with her. It's like getting to keep a trophy for accomplishing something big in life. In my case, once I help Violet, she becomes my reward. I've never worried about any girl the way I worry about her, which makes her the perfect wife for me. My biggest priority is for

Violet to be mine and in the most utterly perfect condition, not just physically but psychologically as well. Step one is healing Violet … consistently.

I tense my jaw at the thought of not being able to have Violet. I've needed her for my medical studies all this time, and now that we are adults, I can make that possible. I work part-time as an assistant in a medical office and, luckily, I have access to it whenever I need it. They gave me the keys because I sometimes stay until late to finish typing the doctor's reports and adding them to the system. The office is closed on Fridays, Saturdays, and Sundays, so I have the perfect opportunity to get Violet in there with me on those days.

"Can't we just bring her over to your office? I mean, what's the point of keeping her hostage?" Elliot suggests.

I roll my eyes at him for the gazillionth time.

Has it ever occurred to him that I've already thought of that?

"Elliot … listen to yourself. She isn't open to the idea of anyone healing her, right? I mean, she's terrified of all things medical."

"OK. Your point?

"If she can barely talk about medicine without squirming, then how the hell do you expect her to come to my office willingly?"

Elliot paces around. "Then that should be our focus question."

I remain quiet, challenging his gaze.

"Well?" I finally say. "What should we do?"

Elliot's eyes light up. "Give me some time with her. All she needs is a little push. So far, she trusts me, and that's a start."

I cross my arms. "How do you expect her to stay once she sees me in scrubs ready to give her a physical?"

Elliot pats my back and sighs. "Leave it to me. I've got this."

What's interesting is how Elliot is so sure about getting our plan to work when he doesn't even know the plan itself. I know that the real reason why he is trying so hard to help me is to get Violet all to himself for his own medical studies. That or he just really likes her. He has the same intrigue as me, only I'm apparently more "obsessed," as he likes to call it.

He picks up his phone and opens the call icon.

"What are you doing?

He faces me. "Just gonna make a quick phone call."

I place my hand over his phone. "No. First, you'll tell me what you're gonna say to her."

Elliot inhales. "Just let me call her. I'll know what to say once I start."

I let his phone go. "Then do it."

"Put her on speaker," I whisper over the sound of the phone dialing.

The call connects. He presses the speaker button.

"Hello?"

"Hey! Did you get home safe?" Elliot asks.

"Yeah, thanks for asking. I'm actually about to get in the shower right now."

End the call, I mouth to Elliot. His eyes signal to me that he understands.

"Oh, that's fine. Um. I was just gonna ask you if you're down to go for coffee with me tomorrow morning."

I nod. I like where Elliot is going with this.

The sound of the shower being turned on emerges from the phone.

"Oh, I'd like that," Violet replies. I hear the excitement in hear voice and imagine she's beaming. Good.

"I'll pick you up at ten?"

"Sounds like a date." She giggles.

"Great, see you then!"

The call ends.

"What are you planning on telling her tomorrow?" I ask.

Elliot stretches his hands behind his head. "We'll see when tomorrow comes."

"*What?* You can't just go into this without a proper plan in mind."

Elliot pinches the bridge of his nose and shuts his eyes. "Just trust me. It'll come to me naturally. Besides, how am I supposed to predict her reaction?"

I sigh. "OK, Elliot, but You're going to be geared up with listening devices again."

"As usual," he utters sarcastically.

I smirk. "Hold up, I have something in mind."

"What do you mean?"

"I know exactly what you should tell Violet tomorrow," I say. "Listen carefully ..."

4

Violet

I catch a glimpse of Elliot's black Mercedes through the first-floor window as it pulls up to my house. A message from Elliot pops up on my phone.

Elliot: I'm here :)

My cheeks flush as I walk out the front door, nearly tripping over my feet for the second time this week. I really hope Elliot didn't catch that. "Hey, stranger," I joke.

He beams as I get in the car. "You ready?" He turns up some pop music as he pulls away from my house.

"Uh, yes. I'm in desperate need of caffeinated tea this morning."

"Same here." He fakes a yawn.

This ride feels like a minute away from my house, but I wouldn't know the difference, as I was too occupied enjoying Elliot's company. As our destination comes into view, I'm not surprised to see he's done it again. *Wow,* I mouth.

"I did it again, huh?"

Whoa, it's almost like he read my mind.

I elbow him. "No, seriously. Wow. How do you do it?"

"You'd be surprised what a few clicks on your keyboard can find."

I look out upon the whole floor as it is swarmed by server bots at our service. We follow one of the server bots to our table. The bot places two menus on our table.

"Wow, this is very nice."

He chuckles. "Yeah, this is the third time you've mentioned that. I love it too."

I clear my throat sarcastically. "So. What are you thinking of ordering?"

Elliot picks up his menu, looks at it for a split second, and puts it down.

"The powdered waffles."

"Did you even read the menu?"

"Eh, I already knew what I wanted to order before we sat down. I come here a lot."

I narrow my eyes dramatically. "I see."

"And what about you?"

"Scrambled eggs."

Elliot presses a button on our table to call the server bot, which shows up in seconds.

"We'd like scrambled eggs and powdered waffles."

"Any drinks?" The bot's voice sounds so human-like.

Elliot eyes me.

"One tea."

"That will be all," Elliot tells the bot.

The bot shows up with the tea in less than a minute.

My eyes widen. "High-class service."

I sip my tea, nearly burning my tongue.

"Did you reschedule your appointment?"

I hesitate. Wow, he's already getting straight to the point. "What appointment?" I ask, as though I don't know exactly what he's referring to.

"Well ... you know. Yesterday. You said that you ditched it to go on a date with me instead."

I chuckle. "Oh, that? No, I didn't. Why do you ask?"

"As a doctor in the making, I would hope that you're prioritizing your health. Wouldn't you?

"Yeah," I smile insincerely, "but I was thinking of switching to another doctor anyway."

He raises his brows. "Why? What's wrong with yours?"

Elliot sort of looks relieved by my response, which surprises me.

"I'd rather not talk about it." Translation, *I'd rather not make a complete fool of myself.*

"Look, you don't even have to switch over. I have a better idea."

Oh, I really want to hear his proposal. "What are you implying?"

"I can bring you to a place where you can get a doctor's visit completely *free* of charge."

That sounds too good to be true. "Really? What kind of joke is this?"

"I'm serious. I can bring you over there, and you can tell your mom that you actually went without it being a lie."

He's not convincing me. The real question is, *Why does it matter to him so much?*

"Oh. You're saying free because you think my health insurance will cover the fees."

Elliot crosses his arms and shakes his head. "Nope."

I sigh. "I just applied to a job near the gym, and the

application papers say I need my doctor to complete a health form before being approved."

He leans in. "When did you apply?

"This morning. I applied online, and now I don't really have a choice. I *have* to go to the doctor."

He's trying so hard to hide his smile for some reason. He puts his hand on top of mine.

"Bingo. Here's another reason you can avoid going to your not-so-good doctor and let me take you to one that will see you for free."

There's no way this can be real. "But why is it free?"

"Because my relatives won't charge my girlfriend. I wouldn't allow it."

I melt into a puddle. *Girlfriend.* He said it. That's it … I'm off the market. I'm sold.

"Girlfriend?" I responded flattered.

"Uh-huh. So, what do you say? Would you let me do this out of my care for you?"

I don't even care that I have a doctor's appointment awaiting me. I finally have a boyfriend … and it's him. *Oh my* gosh, this is really happening. Hold up … there's just one problem.

"Wait. What about Adam?"

"What about Adam?" he parrots back.

"Like … won't he get upset? He did like me at one point."

Elliot averts his eyes and chuckles. "Don't worry about it." I catch a smirk spreading across his face.

"Great. So, when do I go to this appointment?"

"How about after we have breakfast?"

"Sounds good." I'm still smiling. I can't help but have mainly one thought in mind. *He* wants *me.* No wait … he *has* me. The only dilemma now is not making a fool out of myself once I'm actually there. If anything, Elliot will wait for me in the waiting room. I hope so.

The server bot brings our plates of food just in time. Our journey to the doctor awaits, and it's only a meal away.

5

Violet

I FEEL LIKE I'M ABOUT TO FALL INTO A FOOD COMA AFTER THAT perfect breakfast.

"I'm surprised that I was able to carry my stomach out of that café." I exhale dramatically.

"*Pfft!* You barely finished your scrambled eggs," Elliot says.

I scrunch up my face. "Yeah, it's a nasty habit."

"Someone's gotta train you to finish your meals." He glares at me, but he's smiling.

"Eyes on the road, Mister."

He looks back toward the road with one hand on the steering wheel. Gosh, he's so hot. I've already melted.

"We're almost here."

"Is it just me, or is every place you take me around the same area? I swear, we haven't even driven a full five minutes."

"That's 'cause it's only been two minutes. Another minute to go. And yeah, that is oddly interesting. Everything is nearby." He shrugs.

At this point I would be nervous, but I'm with *him* and there's nothing that can ruin that. I take that back—we've just pulled up to the place and parked the car. Am I really going through with this? I don't even know who the doctor is. Either way, I don't have a choice. I need the doctor to fill out the health form for my job.

"You ready?"

"Mhm," I managed to squeak. I can barely speak with such a dry mouth.

Elliot's face is glowing with exhilaration. What's gotten into him? There's nothing exciting about taking someone to get medically checked.

My armpits suddenly begin to sweat. My skin is burning up from the inside out. That's the anxiety talking. I think it's my body's way of telling me that I am going to hate this, and absolutely none of this is news to me. This is how I would've felt yesterday if it wasn't for my ditching my appointment.

"You've got this." Elliot pats my back as he leads me into the doctor's office.

The scent of alcohol pads and hand sanitizer nearly kills my nose. Yep, a typical medical office.

The walls are painted pink, which I've heard has a calming effect on patients that tend to be nervous. I can definitely see why that's true. The office is almost like a ghost town ... nobody is here.

I force a chuckle. "Oh, I see what's going on. Are you the one that's gonna give me a physical?" I say jokingly.

"Not at all." He looks serious.

"Oh. Then who is?"

Elliot isn't smiling anymore. He's remaining serious, which causes my nerves to act up again.

"You'll see." He gestures toward the chairs in the waiting room. "For now, just take a seat here."

"You're not gonna sit?" I asked skeptically.

Elliot walks over to the front desk, where there seems to be no one there.

"Actually, I'm gonna have to take over the secretary's desk while you're here."

I stand up abruptly. "Elliot, what's going on? Why is nobody here?"

"That's because you're the only patient today, but don't worry, the doctor is here. He's just in the exam room preparing for you."

My tone gets more serious. "No, Elliot. Take me home. I'm not gonna do this."

All of this is way too suspicious, and I'm really starting to question why he brought me here.

Elliot raises his voice. "I'm not taking you back. I made a promise to bring you here, and I will stand by it."

"Actually, no promises were really made," I retorted.

"Violet. Please. Just take a seat ... I'm not taking you back until you do this. This can only benefit you."

I walk further back. "Fine. Then I'll leave."

Elliot steps away from the front desk. "Go right ahead."

I try to open the door, but it's locked.

"Elliot, unlock the door," I tell him, and my voice holds sternness and panic.

"Not a chance."

Elliot approaches me, showing off the keys in his hand.

"I already told you. No one is leaving until you get examined."

I rebel, "And why the hell does this matter so much to you?" I scream.

The doctor walks into the waiting room. "Because I ordered him to," the doctor says sternly.

No ... not just any doctor ... Adam. It's Adam in scrubs. He is my doctor?

"What the hell?" My voice fades.

I back away slowly in the direction of the nearest and only exit, which is locked.

"Help!" I scream.

"Nobody can hear you." Adam rolls his eyes.

My vision blackens, and my ears are ringing. One thing leads to another, and I'm on the ground.

I'm still conscious although my head is heavy.

I can hear the panic in their voices as Adam and Elliot surround me.

"She's passed out!" Elliot screams.

"Well do something, you idiot!"

"I thought you wanted to heal her."

Someone's lips lock with mine, and each breath seeps into my lungs more and more deeply. I can feel my clothing being stripped off my body down to my underwear, and I start to feel cold. The cold fingers on my body aren't helping.

I slightly open my eyes, seeing two heads looking down over me.

"Violet, can you hear me?" Elliot asks.

"Your blood sugar dropped," Adam adds.

I attempt to sit up, even though my head is still sort of heavy. *Wow, they didn't even do anything, and I've already passed out. I couldn't help it … I panicked.*

I am a hostage trapped in my worst nightmare: the medical office with the most terrifying person in existence. I should've seen this coming, but this is only something any regular person would think of as a worst-case scenario. This is my twisted reality.

"Let's go into the exam room. Elliot, grab her other arm."

I feel weak anyway, so what choice do I have? I find myself

in a room surrounded by tabletops, an examination couch, and a bunch of medical supplies everywhere.

"Sit up on the examination table."

Adam points to it.

Now that my senses are seeping back to me, I've just noticed that I am wearing a hospital gown. Why am I allowing any of this to happen to me?

It's either because I still feel weak from passing out or I've given up too soon. It's not like I can just run away. The only exit is locked.

"We'll weigh you after we do the important stuff first."

I've always felt super awkward around Adam, and here we are in a situation that can't possibly get any more awkward.

"Why are you doing this?" I manage to say.

Adam holds my shoulders and looks into my eyes.

"Listen closely. If you don't do everything I say, there will be painful consequences."

He gestures with his head to the long-needled syringe on the countertop.

"Do you understand?"

I nod desperately. Maybe I should avoid making conversation for now. He's really not in the mood, and I've never seen him this serious before.

My eyes focus on that syringe like my life depends on it. I can only imagine what he'll do to me with it.

Adam grabs the throat scope and the tongue depressor.

"Open your mouth and say *ahh*."

I back away. "Can we not use the tongue depressor? I don't wanna end up gagging."

"You'll be fine. Open your mouth."

I swerve my face away. If I lose my breakfast on Adam, I

just know that syringe will be the last thing I feel jabbed into me before I pass out.

Adam rolls his eyes. "If this is how you wanna behave ... Elliot. You know what to do."

Elliot approaches me and straps me down quicker than I can realize what's going on. Thick, blue, rubber-like straps are holding me down tightly to the examination table. My heartbeats increase drastically.

"Elliot! Please, no—stop!" I panic. I attempt to wiggle out, but there's no escaping.

"I'm gonna ask you one more time to open your mouth and stick out your tongue." Adam's voice becomes sterner.

I stare at the tongue depressor, my eyes expanding, and I ignore Adam's order.

He stretches the mouth opener onto my lips, which keeps my mouth open firmly. Elliot holds my head in place. I hate that I can't turn my face away. Adam shines the light into my throat and lowers my tongue very lightly with the tongue depressor. I can barely feel the tongue depressor, but I can taste the wooden texture. He removes the mouth opener.

"See? That wasn't so difficult."

Elliot unstraps me, and Adam quickly shines a light in my eyes and then my nostrils. I think what makes my situation even weirder is knowing that Adam is still a teenager and he's one year younger than me. So, it doesn't make sense why he would care to do this to me at such a young age.

"So, what's next?" I ask

Adam puts the stethoscope in his ears.

"I'm gonna listen to your heart."

I pull away. "No, I mean once you do the physical. You're really trusting me to come back? Because after this, there's no way I'll agree to be with you."

Should I regret saying that? What if he decides to keep me hostage longer? Then there will really be no easy way out. Besides, I just took a bold risk saying that to someone who stripped me of my power in this small medical office.

Adam takes the stethoscope out of his ears and stares at me like what I said made him realize something. Well, that took a turn. It can't be that easy. I didn't think it was even possible to get through to him, but here it seems like I succeeded. Or not?

Adam pulls his medical gloves off, continuing to stare at me unwaveringly as he does.

He moves toward my ear and says, "Go change back."

Wait … what does he mean by change back? "Like, change back into my regular clothes?"

Elliot picks up the bag behind him and hands me my clothes from it.

"Mhm." Adam nods, finally looking away from me.

I don't dare question him further. Whatever changed his mind is a miracle I don't want to screw up. They both turn away. Again, this undeniably surprises me. Why be all respectful now? I slip out of the hospital gown and change back into my clothes.

"You can turn around now. I'm done."

Adam approaches me so closely that I can feel his hot breath on my face. "Let's strike a deal."

I swallow hard. I didn't expect that. "I'm listening."

"What if I told you I won't give you physicals anymore unless you ask for it?"

I nearly laugh in his face. That was so out of the blue. As if I'll ever allow myself to go through such awkwardness again.

"And why would I do that? There's no way I'll ask you for it."

Adam grins. "Actually, I guarantee that when the time is right, you'll beg for it."

"You're ridiculous for saying that. It's a deal." How random. Beg him for it? I don't think so.

"Not yet. Fortunately for me, both parties have to get what they want in the agreement, so that's not all there is to the deal."

I look over at Elliot, who also seems like he doesn't know where Adam is going with this.

"Go on ..."

Adam leans into my complete focus. "You must agree to go out with me."

I can't help but laugh ... again. Go out with him after everything he just put me through? *Pfft!* He wishes. They stare at me in complete seriousness.

"Is that all? What's next? Do I have to promise I'll give you my hand in marriage?"

Adam's hands squeeze into tight fists as his mouth presses into a thin line. "The choice is yours."

"And what if I say no?"

"Then you'll spend the rest of your days regretting that decision. Take my word for it." His voice is cold and stern.

I swallow hard. "It's sad how this is the only way you could think of getting a girl. No wonder you're desperate."

"Look around, Violet. Do you see any of your friends here to protect you? Perhaps anyone that can stop me from forcing my hand on you?"

My face feels like it's losing its color, but I remind myself to keep my cool. If I continue to show that I'm scared, they will have more power over me.

I clear my throat. "I'll accept your deal, but just know that you forced me into it."

"I did no such thing, but believe what you want. From now on, things will be different between us."

I force a chuckle to assert confidence. "What's that supposed to mean?"

I notice how silent Elliot has been this entire time. Should I be concerned?

"It means that, tonight, we're going out together."

Ridiculous. Imagine having a guy try to woo you after keeping you hostage in a medical office for an entire hour.

"Whatever you say, but once this date is over, that means I've done my part of the deal, and I don't want to see you again."

Adam smirks. "We'll see about that."

"OK, um, I'm gonna take her home now?" Elliot says, bursting with impatience.

I can tell he wants out of here just as much as I do. That doesn't explain why he would agree to bring me here in the first place.

"Yeah, I'm ready to leave," I add.

Elliot escorts me out and Adam stays behind, thank God. At least I won't have to hear from him until later on. Now that we are back in Elliot's car, the energy isn't the same as it was before the doctor's visit.

"Put your seatbelt on." Elliot is avoiding eye contact, and I have a feeling I know why.

"I can't believe I agreed to this crap, Elliot. At least now I'll know never to trust you again." I roll my eyes to add to my heated tone.

"Look I'm sorry ... I ... I didn't mean for this to happen. I feel bad that I—"

"Didn't mean for what exactly to happen?" I interrupt, shouting. "You betrayed my trust, and you know where that gets you? That gets you far from being in a relationship with me, which you so convincingly portrayed! Oh wait ... or was that just an act as well?"

Elliot's face is red, yet he's focusing on the road quite well.

"No, you don't understand. I was forced into helping him. You don't know what it's like with him!"

I look out the window, facing away from him and his pathetic lies. I don't want to talk to him right now. Not when every word out of his mouth is nothing but deceit.

It's silent now. The only sounds are the cars driving past his car.

He breaks the silence. "I don't suggest backing out of Adam's deal. You know … like ghosting him and not going out on that date, 'cause I know that's what you're planning. Honestly, I would wanna do the same, but trust me, it's not worth Adam's temper."

"I wasn't going to not go. I'm well aware that Adam won't let me get away without facing some consequences first. He seems like that type of person anyway."

Elliot side-eyes me and grins like he thinks I'm lying to him. "Right. Like you totally wouldn't ditch him like your last doctor's appointment."

I roll my eyes at his comment.

"In all seriousness, if you don't take whatever deal you have with him, he won't take it lightly. Heck … for all I know, you could end up back in that office and without mercy this time."

"Yeah, Elliot! And that's exactly what you were willing to put me through, you traitor!"

Elliot makes that last turn to reach my house. We're seconds away.

"OK. You're mad, and I didn't expect anything different, but I'm on your side … when he's not around."

"That's the stupidest thing I've heard. You know what, just stop the car."

"But your house is half a block away"

"I'll walk," I retort.

Elliot ignores me and drives up to the front of my house.

"You're welcome." He smiles mockingly.

I step out of the car and slam his door shut. I'm not gonna bother saying goodbye to him. He doesn't deserve to hear from me.

All that I can think of doing is hitting the shower and washing Adam's nasty scent off me. I feel like I'm still soaked in the stench of the doctor's evil lair. Yeah, that name suits their office perfectly.

Either way, I wouldn't get the cops involved with what I just went through, because I have no evidence of anything, and I'm sure it would be his word against mine. I'm gonna deal with this the way I believe is right, which means getting this dumb date with Adam over with.

6

Adam

IF I WOULD'VE KNOWN VIOLET WOULDN'T SHOW UP TO OUR date, I'd have kept her trapped in the medical office to this very moment. But no. I trusted that bitch, and here I am paying the price. I've been waiting in this restaurant for over twenty minutes, and every minute has been dreadful. The server keeps impatiently approaching me and asking me to give up the table to the people waiting in line. I guess this date will be a lot shorter if Violet decides to show up right now. This place may not be the talk of the town or as impressive as where Elliot would think to bring her, but it's good enough for what I have planned. In just minutes, the paid actors that I hired will be here, which will be a failure if Violet isn't here before then.

Well, would you look at that? Scratch that—I spoke too soon. Who decides to suddenly show up, but Violet? Violet is wearing a blue off-the-shoulder bodycon dress with black one-inch heels. I'm surprised she bothered dressing up for the occasion, but I'm not complaining.

"Sorry, I'm late. Your brother had to stop for gas."

"How convenient. Of course, he did," I say sarcastically.

"But I'm here now, and for the record, I'm just here for the free meal."

I sneer at her playfully. "Ready to order?"

"Yep. I've been here before, so I'll just get the salmon with mashed potatoes."

Great. This isn't her first time here. I'm not worried though, because, less than a few minutes from now, my paid actors will do my bidding.

"And I'll get the brussels-sprout sandwich," I say.

She sneers. "Yeesh, that doesn't sound so good."

"Why? You don't like brussels sprouts?"

"Actually, I used to love them until I overate them, and now I can't even look at a brussels sprout without squirming."

That was unexpected but so worth hearing about. If I were to keep her captive, I'd feed her brussels sprouts to make her experience more miserable.

Not that I'm planning on keeping her like that, because if this plan works, which I have no doubt about, she's gonna beg to be by my side. Too bad I didn't think of this sooner.

The waiter finally approaches.

"What can I get for you today?"

"The salmon dish and the brussels-sprout sandwich please."

He takes the menus, and I put my hand on top of Violet's to massage it.

"I must say, you two are the finest couple here tonight."

Violet pulls her hand away. "Actually, we're just friends hanging out."

I stare at her in hopes she gathers that I'm pissed off by her dumb response.

"So, Violet, did you get accepted for that job you applied for?"

She sighs. "Nope. I didn't get that health form filled out ...

and I'm not gonna get it filled out from you, no matter what you say."

I shrug nonchalantly. "I wasn't gonna say anything. I already told you that I won't force you into any physicals. It's *your choice.*"

She rolls her eyes. I'd smack her for that if it wasn't for my plan to make her want me.

Suddenly, three girls are running up to our table. My plan has begun.

"Adam? Oh my gosh, stop. No. I can't believe it's really you."

"*Nicole?*" I chant. "What are you guys doing here?"

"We're just having a girls' night out," Brianna says, "but we didn't expect to see you here. Oh my gosh."

Nicole hugs me passionately. "I'm forever grateful to you for what you did for me. I feel like, for something like that, I owe you big time."

Violet is shocked, looking back and forth between me and the girls.

"Hold on, what did Adam do?" Violet asks.

Clarissa shoots her a surprised look. "You mean ... you don't know?"

Violet shakes her head.

"Adam saved Nicole's life. Nearly everybody knows this. Without him, Nicole would've died."

Violet stares at me skeptically. "What do you mean? How did he help her?"

Brianna elbows me. "Oh my gosh, Adam! How did you not tell her? Nicole was very ill, and without Adam's medical knowledge, she wouldn't have known that what she had could kill her. He healed Nicole."

I shrug. "It's true, girls, but I promise what I found was merely an accident."

"Oh, come on, Adam! Don't act so humble now. We're so proud of what you've done for our best friend."

I can tell that Violet is at a loss for words. This is perfect.

Nicole holds out her phone to take a selfie with me, and Clarissa does the same.

"Seriously, you are so lucky to be going out with such a great guy. It's not every day you find someone so devilishly handsome and heroic." Brianna laughs.

Violet smiles and looks at me. "Well, I'm sure Adam is great at what he does."

"Adam, can we all hang out together tomorrow? We should really catch up." Nicole beams. "After all, I wouldn't be here if it wasn't for you, and we never got the chance to celebrate with you."

Clarissa nudges Nicole. "Nicole, we can't tomorrow. We have classes."

"Oh, right. Adam, is there a chance we can chill tonight?"

I look over at Violet and make a sympathetic face. "Look girls, I'm here on a date. I can't tonight."

Clarissa grabs my arm. "In all honesty, I need you for something. You may have helped Nicole, but I want to make sure that I am healthy as well."

"Can't you just go see a real doctor?" Violet interrupts. She has a resentful look on her face.

Nic0le gives her a dirty look. "Girl! You know how many doctors I've gone to, and none found what I have. But meeting Adam was an accident that I will forever cherish."

Suddenly, a guy walks up to our table.

"Yo, Adam, bro! Whassup, dawg?"

"Hey, Martin, I'm just chilling. How are you?"

"Sorry, I don't mean to interrupt, it's just that I wanted to tell you how much your treatment worked. I mean, it's insane, dawg! My arm can actually move without being in excruciating pain."

"Of course, man! Any time."

The girls look at me and start acting jealous for my attention. Nicole blocks me with her body.

"Um, not to be rude, but you're kinda interrupting. We got here first to talk to Adam."

"Well, damn, chill out, would ya?" He moves to where he can see me behind Nicole. "I'll ring you up, Adam!"

"Yep, talk to you then," I respond.

The waiter shows up with our food. "Whoa, it's a whole party over here," the waiter jokes.

"Yeah, Adam here saved my best friend's life."

"You're kidding!" the waiter chirps.

"Nope. He's that amazing." Brianna beams.

"Wow. Congrats, dude. That's a really big deal." He fist-bumps me.

At this point, nearly everyone in the restaurant is watching us as I am being showered with admiration.

I must admit that even though all this attention is fake and paid for, it feels very empowering. In fact, these actors did such a great job that I even forgot that they were acting.

"Well, we've gotta get going, Adam, but check your messages!"

"Yeah, we don't wanna lose contact with you!"

They leave the restaurant, and my attention is back on Violet.

She looks at me like she just witnessed a celebrity in front of her.

"Wow. Adam, I have no words."

I laugh. "Yeah, that was something."

"No, that's incredible. You must be helping so many people and you're not even a doctor yet."

I check my phone making it seem like I got a message.

"Hey look … I'm really sorry, but I've gotta cut our date short for tonight."

"Why, what happened?" Her eyes grow desperate.

"I don't wanna let those girls down. One of them thinks she may have a medical problem that only I can fix."

"So? If it's that bad, she can go to a hospital."

"Well in her case, she doesn't have health insurance and it's not easy for her to pay it off. That's why I'm a big help to her."

"What about the other girls?" she asks.

"They don't have health insurance either."

"Can't they just get health insurance or maybe wait till tomorrow to see you?"

I give her a skeptical look. "Why are you suddenly so interested in their business?"

She swallows hard. "I just thought …"

"It's fine; you don't have to explain yourself, but I really should get going. Let's reschedule?"

Violet nods eagerly. "Yes, of course. For when?"

"Actually, just send me a message and I'll respond with the details for our next date."

I give her a warm smile.

The waiter comes with the check to our table.

"I'm guessing the waiter overheard us," I say.

"I guess so." She laughs.

I place my card with a cash tip, and he takes it and returns my card shortly after.

"Again, I'm so sorry that we barely got to even have the date but until next time definitely," I tell Violet.

She seems disappointed. "Yes, I agree, and it's fine. Things happen."

I escort her out, and she calls a cab home.

Would I say that was worth the hard-earned money? Absolutely.

Would I pass as innocent thanks to this plan?

Without a doubt.

The next step will be to let Violet process all that she has witnessed, and then ... let the mind games begin.

Violet

I just got home from my date with Adam, and the same recurring question is cycling around in my mind over and over again.

What just happened?

Even though I went on that date out of obligation, at the end of my time with Adam, it felt like anything but an obligation. I absolutely hate those girls for making Adam cut our date short. I couldn't care less if they have an emergency, and I'm sure it can wait until tomorrow. In fact, they seemed perfectly fine to me, other than their heart-shaped eyes and drooling mouths over Adam. Even though I'll probably never forget how he kept me hostage in that medical office, today changed things. Maybe he's not as horrible as I believed him to be. Adam is a good person who seems determined to get to the bottom of what is going on with a person's health. I'm betting that he had nothing but good intentions and was worrying about my well-being, which I still feel weird about. There were many people who seemed to recognize him and thank him for healing them last night, and that says something about him. He must really care about people. That doesn't change the fact that I would never feel comfortable allowing Adam to give me a physical. Too bad he made that deal with me, because I'm not giving in no matter what. I can't stand that I actually want to get to know Adam. Before arriving at the restaurant, I thought he was insane if he thought that I'd just easily let go of what he put me through and accept him on this date—until those annoying, high-pitched girls showed up. I have to remind myself that he chose *me* to go on the date with. Not them.

Am I conflicted regarding how I should feel about Adam?

Indeed. I have so many questions after last night, and at the same time, I feel like I should be extra careful around him after being held hostage for an entire hour. I mean, what would any other person do in my place? Perhaps move on and ghost him? I think my best and only option is to text him about our make-up date and see what happens from there. I may just regret not blocking him now if this gets me trapped back into that medical office.

I thought last night was the best time to text Adam about our date.

> Me: Hey, Adam! When can we reschedule our date?

I sent that message last night and I fell asleep with no response. Every notification that buzzed on my phone this morning had me on edge. I kept assuming that the next message was him over and over again. At this point, I'm conflicted about whether or not I should call him. Never mind … I don't want to chase him away too soon. He still owes me that date. Or do I still owe him a date? The point is that I shouldn't have to wait all day just to receive his message. Suddenly, another notification goes off on my phone. I highly doubt that it's from Adam, of all people, because so many other people could have texted me just now.

I reach for my phone, and that's when my heart jumps out of my body.

> Adam: I'm outside of your house and I've got something really special planned for us.

My hands are trembling from overexcitement. It's really him. Weird how I can go from wanting to get away from him to being drawn to him within the same week. Should I be concerned?

Lucky for me, I'm already dressed up and ready to leave the house before his surprise message pops up on my phone, so I send a quick reply.

> Me: Adam! What a surprise! I'll be out in a few ;)

I know my message sounds really enthusiastic, but I need him to think I'm interested in him so that I can have my questions answered. I hit send and hurriedly slip my flats onto my feet. This time, I won't be tripping over my own feet before getting into a car for my date, so I'd say I'm finally well prepared.

I quickly sit in the passenger's seat and exhale.

"Ready to go?" He beams.

"You bet! Where are we going?"

He shakes his head. "Surprises are supposed to be fun. You can't know yet."

I giggle. As long as I get my questions answered, surprise or not, I'll get what I needed.

After driving for half an hour, we arrive outside a roller-skating rink. Adam spent so much time talking on the phone with those annoying girls from yesterday that he barely acknowledged my presence in his car. This is supposed to be my time spent with him and, so far, he's been wasting every bit of the time I could be asking him questions. Like, what if those girls were once hostages that he healed and, suddenly, they are grateful to him? No ... I'm being paranoid, I know that, but what other explanation is there? Any normal person would go to a real doctor to get medical help. If paying is a problem, I'm sure it's a possibility to turn up at a hospital if it's really an emergency. This isn't rocket science, so it shouldn't be so difficult for them. How in the world did Adam meet these girls in the first place? It's not like he could just meet them on the streets and ask if they need help medically. Should it be concerning that people are going to see someone for medical help who doesn't have a medical degree? The questions are only piling up, and somehow, I have this feeling that it's not really about being impressed by Adam anymore but more of a potential safety issue. For all I know, Adam could have paid those people to act in front of me. I know that's the paranoia talking, but I can't help it. All that's left to do is spark a conversation with him.

Only as we now enter the roller-skating rink does he finally hang up with the girls.

"So, Adam, how did you meet those girls?"

He holds the door open for me. "Oh, the girls. Um ... I know them from my cousin. So, you see, my cousin is friends with them, and I met them over at my cousin's house."

I nod to show I am following what he is saying. "Go on." I smile, encouraging him.

"And then they went on complaining about their weird

symptoms and how they can't get health insurance. So, I offered to help them out and we went on from there."

Does this information seem too good to be true? Nope. Actually, it sounds pretty believable to me.

"Wow, that sounds great. What about that guy from yesterday who also came up to us?"

He stops walking and turns to face me abruptly.

"You seem to be extremely interested in them. I mean, seriously, what's going on?" He's annoyed, so at this point I'm just going to be honest with him.

"Fine, I'll tell you what's going on. I'm not buying their stories, and honestly, it all just seems too good to be true."

He stares at me in disbelief. "So … what? You think they just lied about all that?"

I cross my arms. "I don't know. You're not a real doctor, so it's a bit too early for you to start healing people." His eyes burn with rage after that last sentence. What's his problem? "I don't mean to be annoying, but this seems very all up in my face and unusual."

We continue walking to the counter, where we are supposed to get roller skates. He's completely ignoring me.

"What's your foot size?" he asks while completely disregarding what I just said.

"Five and a half women's."

"Wow, you've got really small feet."

He hands me roller skates after paying. I'm not getting why he's avoiding my question.

"Do you not wanna talk about yesterday?"

He sighs. "Violet, what happened yesterday doesn't concern me. I'm here with you in this present moment, and I want us to enjoy it."

Maybe he's right. I could be making a big deal out of this,

and maybe he really is that impressive even as a fake doctor. I'm sure that if I don't let this go, he'll make me either way, so there goes the rest of my questions. Down the drain.

"Now. Let's have some fun. Are you ready?" He smirks.

"Actually, I've never done this before, but I guess I'm ready."

"That's perfect," he mutters under his breath.

By the time I get my roller skates on, he's already had his on and been waiting. Once I'm ready, he helps me stand.

He glides around with the skates like it's as easy as walking for him. Meanwhile, I'm holding onto the nearby railing for dear life.

"C'mon, Violet. Don't be scared,"

He comes to me and grips my arm firmly.

"Look, I'll help you." He steadies me and guides me throughout the floor. Wow, this is actually really nice. We're both smiling so big, and the background music that is playing is a huge plus for the experience. So far, it's been a good ten minutes.

"OK, I'm gonna let go now."

"No. No! Please don't," I beg.

I attempt to stand in place but fail miserably and fall, face flat on the ground.

I hear Adam laughing. "You OK?"

I look up to meet his eyes. I feel something dripping down my nose, and panic surges through me when I realize what it is.

"Oh, shoot, you're bleeding from your forehead," he shouts.

This time, there's more concern in his voice but he's still smiling. Is he really making fun of me right now? I don't find being in excruciating pain funny.

"My knees hurt like hell," I grouch.

"You wanna call it quits and get out of here then?"

I scrunch up my face. "Didn't we just get here though?"

He helps me up. "Violet. You're bleeding. I think we should get going. The blood will start to spread more."

Adam guides me through, and as soon as he loosens his grip, I trip and fall on my right hip. The pain from my elbow and hip sends burning sensations throughout my body. Everybody around us turns to look.

I hear someone say, "Ooh, that must really hurt."

Adam tries to hide his smile, but I know he really wants to laugh.

"Ah, crap. I'm so sorry. I didn't think you'd have this much trouble being here."

Jerk. I'm starting to realize that me falling is a great form of entertainment for him. A chuckle escapes his lips as he finally guides me out of the skating area and takes off our skates.

The people that pass me stare and give me sympathetic looks as the blood seeps down to my chin. It burns so bad.

"Adam, I need a cloth or something to wipe the blood. It's dripping all over me."

"Yeah, I have a first aid kit in my car, so I should be able to help you out there."

I roll my eyes. "If this is your idea of me asking you for a physical to see if I'm OK, it's not happening."

He shakes his head as he opens his trunk to get the first aid kit. "Not gonna happen 'cause I wasn't gonna ask you anything. You seem to keep forgetting that you're the one who has the option to ask for it. I don't have to say anything."

I raise a brow at him. "Is that so?"

He opens a rear door of his car and gestures for me to get in. He gets in with me.

Adam pours some kind of liquid onto a cloth and pats it on my forehead.

I flinch. "Ouch, that burns."

"Yeah, it's supposed to do that," he says softly.

It's really quiet, and all that's in my focus are his eyes, which are less than a foot away from mine.

He continues wiping off my blood and patting the most painful areas with the wet cloth. Every pat with the cloth burns more, but I keep quiet.

He slows down, and this time our eyes meet again. Time stops, and my eyes travel to his plump lips and then back to his eyes again. I bite my lip, and before I can take a second to plan my next move, his lips lock with mine. His hand cups my face and slides down to the back of my neck. We keep going at it for a few seconds longer. I never thought I'd have a kiss as long as this one. Especially for a kiss like that, this was one I wouldn't want to forget. When he pulls his lips away from mine, my cheeks burn for a moment.

"Um. That just happened." I look away after realizing what I've done.

He leans in close to my lips, and before I can lock mine back onto his, he whispers, "I missed a spot." He backs his face away and pats my forehead with the cloth again. "There. Just a little more now."

I pull his wrist down slowly. "I think that's enough."

"What's enough?" His voice is velvety and soft as he stares into my eyes without looking away for a second.

"I mean, I've got it from here." I use my phone camera to watch as I wipe and pat the hurt areas of my face with the cloth.

"Violet?" he whispers softly.

I look over at him while I keep patting with the cloth.

"I almost forgot to give you this. Here, take it." He hands me what looks like a turkey sandwich. "I made it for you earlier in case you get hungry."

I freeze as my cheeks heat up for the second time in this car.

"Thanks." I take it from his hand. "Can I eat it here?"

He scrunches his face. "Eh, I prefer you not to, actually."

"Oh yeah. Of course, I'll have it at home instead."

He breaks off the moment and speaks a bit louder. "Right, I've gotta take you back home. Wanna sit back in the front seat?"

"No, it's fine. I'm good back here." I give him a warm smile. The energy around us has changed really quickly, and now it's almost like we are being professional with each other.

"Here, I'll turn up some soft music."

We don't talk the whole ride to my house, and I rest my eyes. I dream of that kiss we shared until I start to feel like I am being carried.

I softly open my eyes halfway to see his chin above me as he carries me up to my front doorstep. I hear my keys jingle as he attempts all three keys until one of them swings my front door open.

"Adam, what are you doing?" I mumble.

"Shh," he says.

I feel like I've been placed on the couch, and I hear the front door close.

Before giving in to the idea of opening my eyes, I doze off.

8

Violet

JUST FOUR DAYS AGO, I WAS AT THE ROLLER-SKATING RINK with Adam, which started off as hell and ended up really pleasant, especially after that kiss that I still haven't been able to forget. I remember waking up hours after I found myself on the couch, and Adam had texted me to tell me that he has another surprise for me for the next day. To my surprise, I was super thrilled about it. When that day came, I had no messages, no calls, no surprise, no nothing. I texted him later that day to ask if the "surprise" had been canceled or what was going on, but I got no response. I thought that maybe he was busy or maybe I should stop lying to myself and accept the fact that I'd been ghosted. I got my hopes up waiting for that day, all just to constantly check my phone to see if he answered while thinking about what he potentially had planned for us.

I've never been more disappointed. He ditched me. Or not. Had something happened to him? Or maybe he had an emergency patient that he had to help at the very last minute. Yeah, that definitely has to be it, since he does take his patients very seriously. He even cut our first date short because of those stupid girls just 'cause they wanted his attention or healing or some other bullcrap like that. Whatever it is, you don't just ghost someone for three days after telling them to look forward to a surprise. I can only imagine that the surprise must be about him disappearing for a few days, because yeah, I'm definitely surprised.

Then, just when I thought I couldn't feel any lower, I saw him. Or rather, I saw his name pop up on a mutual friend's Instagram story. There he was, smiling and laughing, seemingly without a care in the world. Anger and hurt surged through me as I realized he was out there, living his life, while I was left picking up the pieces of my shattered heart.

I want answers, closure, anything to make sense of the mess he left behind. So, against my better judgment, I reach out once again, pouring out my heart out in a message, laying bare my feelings in the hopes that he would finally give me the closure I so desperately crave. There's still no answer.

Maybe I should call him? In fact, that's exactly what I'll do. It's all that I can think of to put my worries at rest.

The phone rings ... it's still ringing ... and would you look at that ... no answer.

I call again ... and again. Then just one more time, in case that will do it. *No answer.* I've called a total of four times. Maybe I shouldn't have done that. This probably only makes me look desperate. Or worse ... obsessed. Am I obsessed? No, I'm not. I'm just confused why he left me hanging for days. I think I'm just attached, which feels really sudden. I do, however, notice that on the fourth call, it says he declined. So, he *is* ignoring me. Wow. I can't believe this crap. Isn't he the one who wanted me first? He went through so much trouble to trap me in that medical office, and now he's just ignoring me? This makes no sense.

Me: Hey, I just realized that I accidentally butt dialed you those four times. So sorry!

I hit send. It's been a few minutes, and my messages haven't been delivered to him.

He blocked me.

Adam

"I don't know, Adam ... this all just feels wrong."

I roll my eyes at Elliot. Does he ever think before saying something? It's been a month since I ghosted Violet, so if she hears from anybody that I'm related to, she'll get even more desperate to hear from me.

"So, what do you suggest? To just throw away my entire plan just 'cause you feel like it's so *wrong*?"

Elliot doesn't respond. He continues typing away for his biology report, not giving a care to what I'm saying.

"Call her." I hand Elliot his phone from the table.

He snatches it without making eye contact.

"I don't know what you expect her to do. She doesn't trust me anymore, and it's not like she will let me in all of a sudden."

"No, Elliot. You're wrong. Desperate times call for desperate measures."

Elliot sneers at me. "Interesting how you have it all figured out, huh?"

"Just call her."

He sighs and dials Violet with a hint of annoyance. He looks up at me and signals that she answered.

"Put her on speaker," I whisper.

"What do you want, Elliot?" she answers.

"Wow, not even a hello? OK, I see how it is."

The call goes silent for a moment.

"Um, so I was hoping I can pick you up later so we can talk," Elliot says finally.

Violet sighs. "If it's important enough, you'll say what you wanna say on this call."

Elliot signals to me with his eyes as if trying to say, "I told you so."

"I wanna meet up with you," he blurts out.

"Fine. When and where are we meeting up?"

Wow, she gave in that quick? I should be surprised, but I guess I'm not.

"I'll be over at your house in a few. We can talk in my car."

"OK. I just don't get why we can't have this conversation over the phone. Isn't it the same as being in your car?"

"Just trust me."

"Mhm. Trust isn't in the cards for you, but I'll take my chances."

Elliot and I get in the car and hit the road while we are still on the call.

"Be ready, I'm almost here."

She exhales, annoyed. "Whatever. Hurry up, 'cause I've gotta be somewhere soon."

"Yes, ma'am."

Elliot hangs up. Now that we're here, that's my cue to get on with my plan.

"I texted Violet to come out. Get out of the car. Hurry!" Elliot snaps.

I step out of the car swiftly. I don't typically tolerate getting ordered around by Elliot, but in this case, I had to listen. "Remember the role you're playing with her. Don't screw this up."

Elliot waves his hand to imply that I should hurry up and leave. I'll be over at the medical office if Elliot texts me that she's given in and we can move forward with my plan.

10

Violet

To be completely honest with myself, I didn't expect to end up back in Elliot's car, but here we are. I didn't even think I'd get a call from him either, after being ghosted by Adam for a month. It was so sudden.

"Elliot, why am I here?"

"You're here because I owe you an apology, for everything, and it's only right if I do it face to face with you."

"So, what? Do you just expect me to—"

"To forgive me? No, I don't expect that," he interrupts, "but I want us to be honest with each other."

I roll my eyes at him. *Honest with each other? That's one hell of a thing to ask for.*

"I'm sure you're aware that Adam ghosted me." I look down to avoid eye contact. The truth is, I'm on the verge of crying at the thought of Adam disappearing after everything. I feel a tear escaping my eye. "So, if you really mean your apology, you'll tell me the truth."

"The truth? All right, then, here it goes. Adam has moved

on. He realized that he doesn't want to force you to go out with him. It's too hard on you."

I want to scream, hit—do something. Is he out of his mind? I should've known his pathological lying is all I'll continue to hear from him.

"Oh, *really*? What's *hard* on me is that he left me questioning my own worth with his sudden disappearance. Was it really so difficult to communicate like a normal human being?" I yelled loud enough that anyone outside the car probably heard me.

"Has it ever occurred to you that maybe Adam feels too guilty to respond?"

I cross my arms and finally lower my voice. "You know what's interesting, Elliot? You seem to have an answer for everything."

The car is now silent. I look out the window and notice rain droplets forming on the glass.

Over a month ago, Elliot and I were drawn to one another like magnets. I remember when there was a spark of joy that would awaken inside of me when we were hanging out before the medical office drama, but the thing is … I don't feel the same for Elliot as I used to. We've lost that spark that made me feel so alive, and something tells me that Elliot feels it too, but now I want Adam.

"Let him go, Violet," he finally says quietly, as though he can read my mind.

I turn to Elliot, and as swiftly as I can, grab his face and kiss his lips. I let my lips massage his for a few seconds more before pulling away.

"I already have," I reply, smiling.

Rebound. That's what I need. Throughout the entire month, I've tried rebounds, but I was never happy with them. This time is different, though, because with Elliot I can make Adam jealous, and he won't resist but come back to me. I guess now I should kiss my date tonight goodbye, because this plan is better.

Elliot's smile suddenly fades. Shoot, maybe I played my part wrong. I need Elliot to cooperate if we are gonna be making Adam jealous.

"Violet. I'm not doing this."

I freeze. My heart nearly skips a beat. I keep quiet.

"I know what you're doing. If this is your way of getting back with Adam, I already told you to let him go. Just accept that he doesn't want you, and I promise you he doesn't care, because the last thing he needs is you annoying him and clinging onto him like a desperate little girl!"

Wow. That's rough. To hear it from Elliot hurts more than admitting it all to myself.

Tears sting my eyes even more than before.

"I'll do it, Elliot ... I'll let Adam give me physicals."

I can't believe those words I have forbidden since the beginning have left my mouth. What the hell is wrong with me? I can't be this desperate. I just can't ... but this is the only way. Otherwise, I'll never hear from him again. Elliot made that clear as day, and I can't be left alone. I really like him.

"What?"

"You heard me."

"Are you sure this is what you want?" He looks concerned, like he is genuinely worried that I've made this choice.

"Yes."

"Well. In that case, I am sorry in advance."

What's that supposed to mean? Elliot sends a message to someone and starts his car. My breathing accelerates as the vehicle moves faster.

"Where are you taking me?" I yell, holding on for dear life.

"We're going to the medical office."

"*What?* Are you crazy? I've gotta be somewhere in ten minutes."

Elliot shrugs. "I guess you should've thought about that before making your decision to get your physical."

I roll my eyes. "I didn't mean right *now*. You know what … I take back what I said. Just take me home."

"Sorry, I can't do that. The deal was struck, and I wouldn't back out if I were you."

If I were you. Those words linger heavily in my mind. He says that as though he knows what I feel right now. How terribly sorry I feel for making that stupid deal on impulse. Maybe moving on is still possible, but now that I said the words that I dreaded most, there's nothing I can do. I would consider backing out and leaving this car if it wasn't moving so fast, but I know better than to get myself in bigger trouble.

Here's the thing—a part of me is only doing this for the sake of seeing Adam again, and a bigger part of me is looking for an escape from this deal.

Conflicting.

If I wasn't so impulsive, I wouldn't have these problems—or better yet, I wouldn't be involved with these wannabes. I guess I won't be needing to go on that date that starts in ten minutes. To be honest, I'm not so interested in that guy I'm supposed to see anyways, but if I were to choose between that and getting a physical examination, then I'd rather choose the dreadful date.

Elliot parks his car right outside of the place I thought I'd never see again.

The interior of the office is just as I remember it. Even though the pink walls are supposed to make an illusion of calm, instead I feel them closing in on me.

"You know what, Elliot? I think I can do this."

I exhale slowly to ease the nerves.

"That's the spirit! OK, go sit in the waiting area."

I do as I'm told, even though it's dumb making me wait if there's literally nobody here today, but I'm not complaining. If there's one thing I'll get out of this, it's some acknowledgement from Adam, and I'd say that's good enough for me. Maybe now I can put him on the spot and make him feel bad for avoiding me. If this is the only way to talk to him, so be it.

"Violet," Elliot calls out. "The doctor is ready to see you. Come right this way."

This feels like roleplay at this point, but I think Elliot is just trying to make this feel as realistic as possible. Maybe to get over my irrational fear of the entire doctor's-office process.

"Step up here with your shoes off."

The weighing scale levels up to 91.2 pounds. I gained a pound. Wow. That doesn't usually happen.

Elliot stares at my numerical weight for a few seconds like he's surprised and then writes it down on his clipboard.

He sighs. "You're five-one. I can't say I'm surprised about that."

"Yeah, but you seemed to be when you saw my weight."

"It's OK. My brother is nearly an expert. He'll know how to help you."

"Nearly," I say under my breath and roll my eyes. I want to say I didn't ask to be here, but then I'd be lying, which makes me the fool. It's fine, this will be over before I know it. It will be my first and last physical with Adam, since it's not like I asked him for it more than once. Right?

I follow Elliot into the exam room and sit up on the examination table. I think Elliot forgot about me having to dress into a gown, but I'd rather not remind him.

Adam, who is wearing blue scrubs and a stethoscope around his neck, walks into the exam room.

He smirks at me. "I'm assuming you know why you're here."

He opens the file that Elliot wrote my height and weight in and raises his eyebrows in surprise once he sees it.

I sigh. "Unfortunately." My voice comes out shakily.

I hope he can't tell that my legs are trembling. I inhale as softly as possible so that it's not noticeable that I'm trying to calm myself down. *Act cool,* I remind myself. To be honest, I don't think I'm in the mood to put him on the spot for ghosting me anymore. There's still time for that.

He squirts hand sanitizer onto his hands and rubs them together vigorously, which makes me more nervous for some reason.

We make eye contact and my emotions take over, forcing me to smile as my cheeks get hotter. I look away as fast as I can and attempt to keep the corners of my mouth down before making a bigger fool of myself.

Adam puts the stethoscope ear tips in his ears and places the chest piece under my shirt.

The stethoscope feels cold on my chest and so do his fingertips. My heart picks up the pace as Adam moves the bell around my chest. He places his hand on my shoulder as he gets closer to me.

"Just relax, I'm only listening to your heart," he says softly, his voice dreamy.

He places the chest piece on my back under my shirt.

"Nice deep breath in for me."

I do as he says, breathing in and out, each breath shakier than the last. I don't know what's more nerve-racking: the fact that his hand is under my shirt and traveling across my chest and back, which is attractive, or the fact that I have feelings for him. I can't believe I had the audacity to think that the last physical was awkward when this one makes me feel all types of nervous, especially the type that invites butterflies to take over my entire stomach.

He looks at me and smiles as he takes the stethoscope out of his ears. "Your heart is beating really fast."

I roll my eyes at him. He obviously said that because he is enjoying how nervous I am right now. It's embarrassing, honestly, but rather than acting as degraded as I feel, I try to hide the nervousness. I must admit that, so far, I'm not doing such a great job of not revealing my anxiety.

Adam shines a light in my nostrils, and I can't even express just how self-conscious I feel as he does that. If I wasn't attracted to him, I probably wouldn't care what he thinks when he checks me in these kinds of areas.

Adam swiftly grabs a tongue depressor while still holding the light with his other hand. My mouth dries out until there's no trace of saliva on my tongue at all. Oh, crap, here we go again. I'm going to hate this.

"I'm assuming you won't make a scene like the last time, right?"

I want to avoid embarrassing myself, so I need to act tough. The cooler I act, the less suspicious he will be about me feeling shy.

"No, I'll do whatever needs to be done," I say as confidently as I can.

"Good to hear. Now open wide and say *ahh*."

I stick my tongue out, closing my eyes as he places the tongue depressor as far back on my tongue as possible. He presses hard on my tongue, awakening my gag reflex, obviously on purpose. Suddenly, my throat spasms, and I start gagging with my tongue still sticking out. He places the trash can under my chin in case I puke, as he looks like he's holding in the biggest laugh ever. I push the trash can away and chug the cup of water that Elliot brings in for me.

Adam is mockingly smiling at me. Making fun of me seems like such amusement for him.

"Are you good now?" Elliot asks, his voice filled with concern. Wow, at least someone cares. Unlike Adam, whom I don't recognize at all right now.

"What the hell is wrong with you, Adam? First of all, tongue depressors are used for children! Not adults. Second of all, you're not being serious at all, which is really concerning," I yell.

Adam nods to Elliot, who takes that as a cue to leave the room. Great, now I'm alone with someone who is clearly enjoying making fun of my fears. He's a jerk, if anyone asks me.

"Look, it's simple. If you're gonna act like a child, then I'll treat you like one."

"A child? Wow, you're really not ready for the medical field if you're gonna criticize me like that, and honestly, you seem childish for making fun of me," I retort.

"I'll be the judge of that," he says sternly. "Now, lay down on your back and lift up your shirt."

Suddenly my self-respect tugs at me to remind me that I still have the choice to talk back, which I wouldn't regret for even a second.

"I don't like that idea. I won't be lifting up my shirt."

Adam crosses his arms. "Oh, really? Then leave—but just know you won't ever hear from me again."

I get silent. His words really sink in every second that passes. He doesn't mean what he just said to me, does he? This time, I'm staring at him in shock, like what he said paralyzed my motive for leaving.

"That's what I thought," he says scornfully.

I feel my eyes burning up with tears, which I'm fighting to

keep inside. If it means I will never see him again, there's no way I'm leaving.

I lay back on the exam table and lift up my shirt below my breasts. Adam presses down on the left side of my abdomen and then travels up on my right side.

"Tell me if you feel pain, OK?" His face looks serious this time. That's the first time he's looked serious today. Maybe it's because he's finally getting to the important stuff.

"OK," I whisper while suppressing my tears.

I feel pain growing deeper the higher he presses on my upper abdomen.

"Ouch. Stop, stop." I squirm.

"You feel pain here?" he asks as he presses on my upper abdomen.

"Mhm," I say, closing my eyes as though it will help ease the pain.

"Interesting."

Adam picks up the clipboard chart and starts jotting some notes down.

I sit up. "Is everything all right?"

"I'm not sure yet. Lay back down." He remains serious.

Adam puts the stethoscope ear tips in his ears and places the chest piece on my abdomen to listen to what's going on inside. This feels so awkward, but I'm going along with whatever he's doing. I'm not just gonna leave after getting this far in the physical. He still owes me a conversation for ghosting me. That's my motive for staying right now. The stethoscope chest piece feels so cold on my belly.

"All right, now we're gonna do some blood work."

I sit up fast in complete panic mode.

"Wait, what? Right now?"

Adam quickly prepares the supplies and puts them on the countertop. "Just relax. It will be quick."

I swallow hard, even though my mouth feels so dry.

"Oh, I almost forgot to do something."

Adam puts his fingers under my neck checking my lymph nodes. That felt really weird.

I exhale shakily. It's getting really obvious how much I'm freaking out right now.

"Give me your arm," he orders.

I obey the command, even though I'm dreading every second of what's about to happen to me. Adam ties the rubber thing around my upper arm and presses down on my vein. Then he opens an alcohol pad and wipes the skin over the vein. I panic and pull my arm away.

"Wait, can I have just a moment to calm down?" I ask.

Adam looks annoyed. "No," he says as he grabs my arm and holds it still.

"Elliot!" he calls out. "Get in here."

Elliot comes in and takes that as a cue to hold me while Adam pokes the needle into my vein, which stings like crazy. A tear rolls down my chin, and it is followed by another tear.

My heart trembles, causing my arms to tremble, which is inconvenient for the blood draw. I don't budge to fling Elliot's hands off me, since I'm not gonna allow myself to come off as childish. I have to prove that I am mature. If I resist the blood draw, then Adam's point will be proven, which would be really embarrassing. I am *not* a child, so I refuse to act like one. Once three tubes are filled with my blood, he pulls out the needle from my skin, and sticks on a bandage to stop the bleeding. Elliot's hands finally let me go, and I exhale shakily, rolling my head back.

"Can I please lay down for a moment?" I ask.

The room spins around, and my vision slightly blackens. Elliot helps me lay back on the exam table and hands me a juice box, which I remember belatedly was also on the countertop. I take a few sips and then take deep breaths in between each sip.

"You'll be fine; just drink your juice," Adam says unsympathetically.

I don't bother talking, since I'm mostly focused on my lightheaded state. I sit up after a few minutes and I feel a bit steadier.

"You OK?" Adam asks, holding onto my leg.

I nod. I feel my cheeks redden, which means the color of my face must be coming back to normal.

I can't help but admire Adam's beautiful eyes. Not to mention his perfect smile. It's weird how I'm only noticing his perfect features *after* those girls went crazy over him. It's like I'm *really* noticing him this time.

"Elliot, I need you to take these blood tubes to the laboratory. Will you make it back in time?"

Elliot checks his watch. "Yeah, I'll be back soon."

"Actually, Elliot, I'll meet you at home. We're gonna wrap this up."

Elliot takes the tubes and leaves.

I'm just slightly more uneasy knowing that Elliot left me here alone with Adam, but I'm managing to keep my composure.

Adam sits down on his wheeled stool and faces me with a serious expression.

"OK, so here's a little health lesson for you. Remember this. The spleen is opposite to the stomach. If the spleen is overactive, the body is likely to be obese, gaining too much weight, and having diabetes. However, if the stomach is overactive, the body is prone to weight loss and not being able to put on weight. Are you with me so far?"

I don't care for what he is saying, but he seems smart for knowing all that just from touching my stomach.

"Um, yeah, I think so."

"Now here's where it gets more interesting, the people with slow metabolisms have overactive spleens compared to people with fast metabolisms, who have overactive stomachs. So, what I'm trying to say is we need to make your stomach work at a balanced rate, which will balance out and slow down your metabolism."

"Wow, Adam. Doctors usually just tell me to eat more, but this is new information," I say, amazed even though I don't really care to memorize what he is telling me.

"We took your blood today to make sure you don't have any vitamin or mineral deficiencies that could also be contributing to your low weight."

I smile. "Adam, thank you. I'm really shocked. I don't even know what to say."

He stands up. Perfect. Now's my cue to ask him. "OK, so now I have to ask. Why'd you ghost me for a month?"

Adam averts his eyes. "That concludes your physical. You can leave now. Please, come back tomorrow for your blood test results."

I follow him out of the exam room.

"What? Adam, this isn't a joke. Do you not care about us? I thought you liked me."

"I do like you, but for now, we can only see each other through these physicals."

He walks away from me, putting his coat on.

"Adam! This makes no sense. I don't get what you want. Why do you care about healing me? I just want clarity," I shout.

Adam ignores me as he packs his stuff.

He doesn't answer me.

"Fine! You know what? I'm not gonna show up to this physical tomorrow if you're being like this to me."

Adam turns to me, and our eyes lock with one another's. "Then don't. It was your choice to come here, and I agreed to help you."

I gasp. "What? My choice? You're the one playing mind games with me and making me want to be with you and receive your physicals."

He smiles at me. "I told you you'd beg for it."

"First of all, I never begged, and you're ridiculous, Adam. I deserve an explanation."

Adam continues ignoring me, as though I didn't just say something to him. I'm shocked at how he is acting right now. He switched up on me so quickly. He leaves through the front door, and I come out with him. He locks the door and walks off after saying, "See you tomorrow," before I get the chance to say anything to him.

I'm sort of intrigued by how Adam did my physical today, and honestly, it wasn't all that bad. I'm conflicted about whether I should come back tomorrow. Maybe Adam is playing hard to get and only told me it's my choice to show up because he *knows* I'll show up just to see him either way. He's clearly an evil genius, which is pretty ironic considering the fact that he is working toward becoming a medical doctor. Who knows? Maybe I'll at least get something out of these physicals and finally gain weight. What I'm really wondering is how much longer will I have to attend these physicals before we can finally date. Hopefully, this ends tomorrow.

11

Adam

SHE LOOKS AT ME EAGERLY AS SHE WAITS FOR ME TO TELL HER the results of her blood test. Yesterday's physical went well, but now that I'm seeing the results, I'm anything but satisfied.

"Well?" she asks impatiently while I stare at her printed blood results.

I sigh. "You seem fine."

Her smile drops. "That's it? I came all the way back to this office just to hear that? You could have told me over the phone."

I know she doesn't mean that. She must be glad to see me physically, since that's the only way to be in touch with me.

"You don't have any vitamin or mineral deficiencies as I thought you would. So, I'll be keeping you on protein shakes to gain weight."

Violet looks relieved. I think I'm making a mistake. How could I be so ignorant? If Violet has no problems for me to heal, and the protein shakes will help her gain weight, then this was all a waste of my time. I mean, of course, I want her to get better, but once I'm done healing her, the fun is over, and I can say goodbye to my dream of continuing to experiment on Violet. I should be getting something out of this too. After all, she owes me for helping her.

"Um, OK. I guess I can try protein shakes. So, are we done here since I'm OK now?"

She looks down to my lips almost like she's drawn to them. Just how I like her, wrapped around my finger.

"Actually, we are just beginning."

"What? But you said—"

"That you're fine? Right, I did say that, but you'll need to come back a whole lot more so that I can track your progress and actually continue to heal you," I interrupt.

Her jaw clenches. "What about after you're done healing me overall? Can we date then?"

It's a shame she doesn't know that the healing won't ever end. I would tell her that, but that will only discourage her from coming.

"I already told you. We can only see each other through physicals."

Violet stands up from the examination table and makes her way to the door.

"Where do you think you're going?"

She turns to me. "We're done here, Adam. I'm out."

My heart trembles out of my body. I know yesterday I said that if she really wants to leave, she can, but that's only because I knew she couldn't resist me. Something has changed. She's really leaving me.

I grab Violet's arm and her eyes widen as she stares at my hand in fear. She shakes my hand off. "Don't touch me!"

"You've left me with no other choice."

I slam her head with the clipboard, and she falls to the ground, her eyes shut.

12

Violet

My eyes are still closed, but my senses seem to seep back to me. I can feel my body on the cold ground and wind blowing on my head. Am I outside?

I attempt to open my eyes and discover a semidark room with dark-gray walls. It almost looks like an abandoned hospital from down here. There's a vent over my head that is creating the illusion of wind blowing over me. It's freezing, but I shouldn't be surprised, since I'm not wearing any clothing. Instead, I have on a hospital gown. I pull my arm toward myself to stretch but find my arms restricted by two sets of handcuffs. My left wrist is handcuffed to the hospital bed to my left and my right wrist is handcuffed to the hospital bed to my right. Panic surges through me as I try to pull my hands through the handcuffs, but there's no use.

"Is anybody out there?" I call out. *"Hello?"*

It's silent. I should've known better and made a run for it when I had the chance, but I trusted the bastard, and here I am suffering the consequences.

"Somebody, help me!" I scream at the top of my lungs.

Something Adam doesn't know about me is the anxiety I've suffered from all these years. I haven't had it flare up in a while, until I got forced into Adam's physicals. Now I have something worse to be anxious about, so whatever he's planning, I don't think I can mentally survive it.

What did he mean when he said I left him with no choice? Is he going to hurt me? No, I doubt it. If his only intention is to heal me, then hurting me is the last thing he would do. No, I take that back. He hit me, which explains the throbbing pain in my head. I'm not safe with him.

Adam finally appears the dim light of the room.

"Adam?"

He doesn't respond. He just stares at me sympathetically.

"Where am I?" I ask, my voice ending strangled from my strong desire to sob.

"Adam, what the hell is going on? Please. *Answer me!*"

"You're in the basement of the medical office," he finally replies.

Oh, good. So, he didn't take me to some sketchy place in the middle of nowhere.

"Somebody, help!" I shout helplessly. "Elliot, help me!" Tears roll down my chin from my desperate, fearful eyes.

"Nobody can hear you." He rolls his eyes.

Wow the déjà vu I feel right now is crazy. This isn't the first time he's trapped me in a medical environment.

He approaches me and caresses my shaking leg. Thankfully, I am able to kick his ankle, and I continue throwing the biggest tantrum I can throw.

"You lunatic! Let me out, you psychopathic freak! You crazy creep!"

I keep kicking my legs around, but he swiftly handcuffs my

ankles together. I really shouldn't have done that. I have no way of defending myself down here.

"I am your doctor—your hero—and this is the thanks I get?"

"Heroes don't imprison those they save, and you are most certainly *not* my doctor!" I scream.

He bashes his fist into my knee at my retort.

"Enough!" his shout silences me. "Now, here's what's going to happen. You're gonna let me heal you down here, and then I might *consider* setting you free."

I sniffle. "Why can't you just heal me upstairs where we just were?"

Adam chuckles. "And take the risk of you walking out on me? Absolutely not."

Oh, I'd do much more than *walk out on him.*

My pulse increases. "You're crazier than I thought, Adam. What are you on?"

"Call me what you want, but that's not stopping me from healing you. I need you, because you need me."

"But why? Why does this matter to you so much?" I sob.

He doesn't answer. He just averts his eyes to the medical bed to my right. He turns on the hospital monitors and approaches me.

I push forward to escape, but the handcuffs restrict me back.

I lower my voice and speak as calmly as I can. "So, that's it? I'm your prisoner now?" I look up at him standing in front of me.

"No. You're my patient that needs my healing. Don't worry, I'll help you just right."

"I don't need your help!"

"Oh, you most definitely need me. You just don't know it yet."

I sigh. "Will you at least release me from these handcuffs?"

"That's the plan, but I need to make sure you'll behave with me, and so far, you're not being docile enough for me to trust you."

I release my tightened jaw muscles and attempt to appear calmer. This might be my only chance at an escape.

"OK, Adam. I'll tell you why I won't run off if you release me: 'cause then I can get this next physical over with, and then you'll let me go right?"

He raises a brow and crosses his arms.

"All right, then I guess I'll release you." He reaches for something in his pocket. I'm guessing it's a key.

Wait, what? Just like that? He doesn't even need more persuading. What a gullible idiot.

He sets my arms free, and I wait for him to unlock my ankles. Now that I'm up, I kick him in the balls as hard as I can, and he bends over screaming in pain.

I run up the steps to the door that will lead me out of the basement, and as I pull it to open, it doesn't budge. Crap. He has the keys.

I feel a needle painfully jab into my upper thigh, and seconds later, I drop and fall down the steps. I attempt to stand up, but I can't feel my numb legs. I'm in trouble.

"That, my dear, was a test. If you wouldn't have run off to escape, we would've done the physical upstairs without restraints, but you failed. You're going to stay here."

I weep heavily. "What did you do to my legs?"

"Relax. It's only an epidural. It will wear off in a couple of hours, which means you won't be running away anytime soon."

"Look, I'm sorry, OK? I'm sorry! I ... I'm just not used to

constant physicals. It sounds so exhausting, and honestly, all I wanted was you. Not the healing." I hug his leg, as I'm still on the floor. "Please, just give us a chance. We can leave all this behind and be together. Please, just let me go, I'm begging you!"

I lied. There's no way I can be with someone as psychopathic as him. I don't care for the attraction anymore; this has done it for me.

Adam chuckles and grabs my chin. "You know, I love it when you beg."

"So, you'll release me?"

"My darling, as someone who is a fan of theater, I can tell you are definitely a theater kid."

Great, he knows I'm acting. That's just fantastic.

Seems to me like the only thing I found attractive about this psycho was his reputation. I mean, why else would I fall for him knowing that he's crazy? Only a miracle could make me love him again. I'm mostly still surprised that all those girls praised him for his help with their health. That's the only thing that's keeping me sane around him.

I'm starting to think that it's not that he wants me to just love him; he already knows I'm attracted to him. No, he wants me to be his guinea pig. I'm guessing it turns him on, since he likes both me and the medical field.

Adam grabs me from under my armpits and pulls me up onto the hospital bed, which is also one of my biggest fears. Since my legs won't be functional for the next few hours, whatever happens will be even more out of my control.

My skin heats up, and my breathing becomes irrationally rapid as I begin to hyperventilate. My wheezing worsens, and there's panic written all over Adam's face.

"What the hell is going on?" he screams. "We need to get another blood test done immediately."

I panic harder. *No*, not the blood test.

"It's my anxiety," I attempt to get my words out fast.

He stares at me. It almost looks like he's annoyed or even disappointed. I can't really blame him, since now he's discovering that anxiety is going to be an obstacle for him during these physicals or whatever it is that he plans to do to me.

"OK, look. Breathe with me. Come on, in through your nose. One ... two ... three ..."

I try to follow what he is telling me to do, but being on a hospital bed is horrific enough, especially due to the irrational fear that I have.

"Good job. Now, breathe out slowly through your mouth. One ... two ... three ..."

My breathing normalizes slightly, and I repeat the process over and over again to keep calming myself down.

"Adam, please don't do this. Now that you see how bad my anxiety can get, can you please excuse me from your healing?"

Adam doesn't respond. Instead, he presses down on my belly and listens to it through his stethoscope.

Next, he listens to my heart with the stethoscope, and I frantically start breathing uncontrollably fast again.

"What's going on now, huh?" he asks sternly.

"I don't want to do this anymore."

"I'm only listening to your heart, if you're gonna keep misbehaving like this, I'll have to chain you down to this bed. Is that what you want?"

His voice is so serious and stern.

I don't find his listening to my heart with the stethoscope attractive anymore. If anything, literally everything he does feels so dreadfully nerve-racking, and I hate how this place looks exactly like a hospital.

"OK, OK, I'm sorry. You can listen to my heart." I doubt that he will get an accurate reading from my heart, since it's beating so irregularly fast. There's no way I'm getting chained down. Wow, and I really thought the handcuffs were intimidating, but it can always get worse.

He continues listening to my heart, placing the stethoscope on my chest and my back. He tickles and caresses my chest, and I flinch.

"Is that also part of the physical?" I ask, annoyed.

He smiles. "You know, I could be doing way worse. You should be thanking me."

"Thanking you? You're just a wannabe doctor whose only chance of healing his patients is by imprisoning them."

Adam sneers and pulls my hair up, which pulls my head upward. So. Much. Pain.

"I don't tolerate that kind of bluntness."

My tears come pouring even more.

"Every time you insult me about not being a doctor, I will display just how much it hurts me by expressing it on you."

He releases my hair, which bangs my head down hard on the hospital bed. There aren't even any pillows, and my head is laying very low. I stay silent, however, fearful that by saying anything else, he'll be triggered enough to keep hurting me.

"Now, I'm gonna be taking a biopsy of your spleen, which means I'll be taking a sample of your spleen tissue using a needle. It will feel uncomfortable, but this needs to be done."

A *biopsy*? Is he out of his mind? He's not a doctor yet. He could easily mess this up! Even if he were successful, there's no way I'm letting him slurp out a sample of my spleen with a needle.

"No, Adam! Please, I'll do anything! I'm begging you, please,

don't do this. Here, take my arm. I'd rather you do the blood test!" I shriek.

God, no ... this is my worst nightmare.

"Scream any louder, and I'll gag you."

He stares at me, waiting for me to scream, but I keep my mouth shut and continue feeling petrified in silence. I couldn't move even if it weren't for the fear that's taken over me. I can't run away, since my legs aren't working, thanks to the epidural.

He takes out a needle for the biopsy and jabs it into the upper right side of my abdomen. I feel like there's a knife cutting away the insides of my spleen—that's how bad the pain level is. I scream and cry while Adam takes a sample of my spleen from my body. My arms tremble, since my legs can't. I'm so tempted to hit Adam, since I have the privilege to have my hands be free, but I know he'll punish me for it, and then he will surely handcuff me again. As he swiftly pulls the needle out of my abdomen, blood squirts out upward, and Adam looks panicked. I'm guessing that wasn't supposed to happen. I cry harder. This amateur college student is going to destroy me with his lack of experience! I really don't want my life to end over a stupid biopsy that this idiot forced onto me. He wipes the blood off with a *tissue*—a freaking tissue—and sticks on a Band-Aid.

"Please, don't hurt me!" I cry, repeating the same words over and over again. "Please, don't hurt me! Please, don't hurt me!"

"*Shut up!*" He smacks my shoulder, and I continue to cry silently. My nose feels hot.

"Look, I'm not going to hurt you! I'm healing you because I love you."

I may not know a lot about love, but I do know that this isn't it.

"Then answer one simple question, Adam. Was blood supposed to just start squirting out of me?"

"No, but don't you see how that's a good thing? This means I'll be healing you longer whenever I make mistakes on you." His eyes widen. "It's experimental, and now that you're all mine, I'll be healing you till the end of time. You get to be healthy forever! Isn't that amazing?"

I stare at him, even more terrified than I was a minute ago. I don't even know if there's a word to describe how insane he is.

"Adam, I don't want to be your guinea pig. There's a reason this is illegal."

Adam squeezes my wrist against my chest. "What did you just say to me?"

I tear up for the billionth time. "I mean, I'm so sorry. I didn't mean what I just said, just please, don't hurt me."

Adam jumps up and down in crazed frustration. "Why the hell do you keep saying that? *I am your doctor—your healer!* I'm not here to hurt you!"

I keep sniffling.

He pauses., before adding dangerously, "But don't take advantage of my generosity, 'cause I could be way worse to you."

I nod at him desperately. "I understand, and I'm sorry."

"The last thing we're doing for today is a urine test. I know you can't move your legs, so I'm going to raise them up for you."

This is so humiliating, and the fact that he is going to see everything … but here I don't have a choice.

It feels never-ending at first, but thankfully, the urination is over quickly. I can't believe that someone I had the audacity to actually feel attracted to is holding a plastic container of my urine right now. It's really baffling how someone can be this crazy.

Elliot shows up in the basement. I've never felt so relieved to see him, and I wish I could give him the biggest hug. I didn't even notice when exactly he got here.

"Adam, can I take her home now?" Elliot asks.

What? This entire time, Elliot knew I was here and didn't consider saving me? Wow, what an absolute jerk. I mean, how could I be surprised though? They are brothers, and I'm nobody to them.

"Wait. You're letting me go?" I face Adam.

"Violet, did you seriously think you're staying here as a hostage? You'll be coming back here every day from now on anyway."

His words linger in my mind. *Every day.*

"Adam, just think about it. What's the point of being healthy if I can't enjoy my good health by having freedom and actually having a life? I don't think daily physicals make sense to do."

"You'll get used to it. Plus, you're getting free healthcare for life, and I get to continue my studies on you. You should thank me."

Adam kisses my forehead. Elliot doesn't react in any way. I assumed that maybe he would express some jealousy, but he doesn't seem to care.

"Elliot will carry you to my house and take care of you for the night."

"But what will I tell my mom? She's going to be so worried about me," I ask, hoping he will let me go home.

"I already sent your mom a message from your phone saying you're sleeping over at a friend's house."

I think I have a plan. Maybe if I gain some more trust, they will let me go home, and then I can finally call the cops on this freak. I just need to have a little more patience.

13

Violet

ELLIOT PUT ME DOWN ON HIS BED A FEW HOURS AGO, AND IT'S been silent ever since. It's getting late, and the day has been so exhausting. After a while, my eyelids started to feel really heavy and I couldn't keep my self awake anymore. As I dozed off, I was unprepared for the memories that would flood back into my mind during this night.

§

Ten Years Earlier

The rhythm of my breathing accelerates as Adam approaches me closer with a butterfly needle in his right hand and three blood collection tubes in his left hand. My legs feel like giving out, but I pick up the pace as I attempt to escape him. One would assume that our school's fitness pacer test would be more helpful in preparing us to run faster, but that isn't the case for me. Not when I'm dealing with the most terrifying human, who could easily be mistaken for a monster. At least, to me he is a monster.

Adam is getting closer.

Looks can be deceiving ... and although Adam doesn't look terrifying, his intentions don't ever feel merciful. I hate that I had the nerve to open up to him and actually have feelings for him ... but it isn't my fault he's so attractive. He's horrifying but exceptionally attractive.

There's no way in hell that I'll let this nitwit fifth grader give me another physical examination. I've counted eight physicals this week, and this is about to be the ninth. What's his problem?

Crazy freak.

Most of all, I'm tired of being constantly held down by all his brainwashed friends. I can't help but end up kicking, shoving, and crying. I mean, any normal person would have that response if they were forcefully receiving physical examinations by a wannabe doctor who's really still a child. Adam is a fifth grader for God's sake ... why would I let him touch me, let alone stick needles into me?

What's Adam's deal with constantly cackling like he is a mad supervillain? It just makes this process so much creepier. I just want to get away from him already. The lunch period is nowhere near over, so this should take a while. For some dumb reason, none of the adults believed me when I told on Adam, and what sucks is how all our peers would side with him and insist I'm making everything up. We both know that Adam paid our classmates and friends to keep quiet about his torturing me, which is so messed up.

His manic cackle consumes me as I reach the interior of the girl's classroom nearly out of breath. I can't handle being chased around any longer. I'm exhausted from running. but by the looks of it, Adam hasn't lost an ounce of energy from chasing me. Instead, it's like he's gained energy.

Gosh, why can't this freak just give up already? I turn to face him as I walk backward slowly. Adam is smiling widely, like a shark that is ready to devour its prey without leaving anything behind. He's cackling again, and that spikes up undeniable fear in my stomach. He looks like he wants to eat me down to my core—bones and all—and I wouldn't be surprised if he did.

Adam's eyes grow desperate the further backward I walk toward the classroom wall. Unfortunately, the classroom is empty so there's no teacher here to stop Adam from doing this to me. Holy crap, his fully dilated pupils are triggering my fight or flight response to go haywire. I'm used to my body reacting this way to him. It's an everyday routine at this point.

"Stop ... I can't ... run ... anymore!" I pant breathlessly. Since I stopped running for a moment, I catch my breath. "Why are you always doing this to me? I'm ... I'm scared."

Adam grabs my trembling shoulder and looks into my tearful eyes. "Ah, Violet. It's simple really. You are my patient, and I am your doctor. Now be a good girl and sit still," he scolds.

"I wanna get out of here! Please, I'll do anything, just let me go!"

Adam smiles wide. "Not a chance," he cackles.

That's it. My legs are completely sore and ready to transform into a puddle of water. I don't have a choice, so I fall to my knees and raise my hand to cover my face. "I'm begging you ... stop! Please. *Please!* Don't do this to me! PLEASE," I whimper.

Adam kneels to level with me. "Look at me. Calm down. No one is hurting you." He makes a serious face.

I squeeze my eyes shut, covering my face with my hands. "Not yet, but you will soon. Just let me go!"

"Don't worry, I won't harm you. I'm only helping you." Adam runs his hand from my thigh down to my knee, and I squirm.

I look back at him while rapidly breathing. Is he not hearing me right now? I wish he would set me free from his daily torture. None of this is news.

I sniffle dramatically, "But you're not a real doctor. You're a child. You ... you shouldn't be doing this to me," I cry.

Crap ... I shouldn't have said that. The last time I said he wasn't a real doctor, he kicked me. Adam's eyes flash with rage, and before I realize what he's about to do next, he smacks me twice with his hand across my back. His fist bashes into my thigh, and a roaring scream escapes my mouth. My tears are making kaleidoscopes in my eyes.

"Next time, I'll beat harder if you say that again."

My heart skips a beat at his threat.

"Out of every girl this can possibly happen to ... why me?"

Adam ignores my question, as though it's dumb to ask that. It's beyond obvious that he likes me—no, he *loves* me, according to my classmates who are also his friends. If love has to feel this torturous, then I don't want him to love me. Who needs love, anyway, if it will feel this dreadful? If this really is *true* love. I'm only in the fifth grade, and I'm not ready for all this love catastrophe. I need a break, and a long one—up until I'm at least twenty years old. Otherwise, I'll fall apart. I can't help the heavy crying or the feeling that my heart will jump out of my chest at any given moment. I want to beg, cry, or scream manically, but I get interrupted before any of that plays out worse than it already has. I think someone is coming to the classroom. I hear heavy footsteps pounding against the floor as though this person is running. Great; this is my perfect opportunity to stand up and run further into the classroom to be away from Adam. I'd sooner trip than escape the classroom so I won't even try. He is blocking the exit, and leaving through there would be a death wish. I don't think he would ever kill me Perhaps hurting me is as far as he would go. I used to think that doctors were good for people, but ever since Adam entered my life, I've believed the complete opposite.

I feel every inch of my body tremble at his presence invading my personal space. Adam is so close that I can feel his hot breath on my face, and it's making me wanna gag.

Adam's friend Eric calls out my name; his voice amplifies closer to the classroom each time.

"Violet …? *Violet* …? VIOLET!"

Oh my. It's about damn time someone is here to rescue me! Plus, this is a great distraction. Every Adam is not able to do a physical on me is very precious. I've never felt more relieved.

We both look in the direction that Eric's voice is emerging from. Eric runs in, panting like a dog and holding a bag of supplies, medical gloves, and a stethoscope. Ugh. Eric is here to help … but I'm not the one he's helping. He is gonna be holding me down, as I should've suspected. This is so freaking dreadful.

"Here, Adam, you almost forgot these."

Eric's face is struck with fear when he sees me on the floor trembling. He hands Adam the medical supplies and gestures to me. I still don't get how Adam gets people to agree to do this to me. I know money is involved, but that can't be all there is.

"Thanks. Hold her down while I prepare," Adam orders.

What surprises me is that there isn't a group of people holding me down like last time. Oh. Never mind. A group of girls makes a sudden visit to the classroom. Fantastic! Now Claudia and four other girls who held me down the last time are here too.

"Hey, we came as soon as we could! Monica had to finish something, so we waited for her," Claudia announces.

"Yeah, that's nice, just hold her the way I taught you to," Adam orders sternly.

"Why so hostile?" Amira jokes.

My intense sobbing feels like it's elevating more out of control now that there are six people holding my arms, legs, and waist. I am entirely overpowered, and all that's left to do now is to receive yet another physical. Gosh, I'm so tired of this. One would think I'd be used to being restricted and forced into all this crap, but I'll probably never get used to it.

There's nothing tolerable about a wannabe doctor sticking a needle into me, checking me, or any of the other stuff that he does in every physical examination.

"Help! Somebody, help! *Aah!*" I shriek while attempting to wiggle out, but every attempt to escape is a failure.

Eric gags me with a cloth, and I listen to the girls chattering.

"Look, it's OK. We'll be done soon!"

"We're almost done. It's OK!"

"It won't hurt. He will be done soon!"

"Don't cry, honey, you're doing great."

"You're doing such a great job. He's almost done, don't be scared."

They are all trying to reassure me through my crazy weeping, while I'm still attempting to wiggle out of their clutches. I feel the stretchy band getting tied around my arm … oh no … it's time for blood draw.

"Don't be scared. It will only hurt a little," Adam reassures me while cackling.

How can I trust him if he is not acting serious while taking my blood? I feel the cold of the alcohol swab on my arm. Then, I feel a needle poke into my arm, and I get silent. I don't want to risk moving around too much. Besides, I'm too late. Adam is already drawing my blood, and I can't do anything to stop him. He has an evil grin plastered on his face, and his pupils expand even further as my blood flows through the tube. Time has never gone by slower. It's suddenly so quiet that I wouldn't be surprised if I heard a pin drop.

After what seems like forever, he releases the elastic band, and I feel the needle being removed and his fingers putting pressure on where he jabbed me. This is followed by a bandage being stuck on. Ow! That was so freaking painful!

"See, that wasn't so bad, and we're all done," Amira says in a belittling voice like she is talking to a baby. I can't even begin to express how power depriving that feels. Do his friends not have souls?

Eric removes the gag cloth from my mouth, and I briefly gasp for air.

"What will you do to me now?" I ask, my voice trembling with fear.

Adam holds out an injection syringe. "Hold her tighter!" he orders.

A shot? *No*, I can't do this ... I just can't. I scream as roaringly loud as I can to attract help from outside the classroom, but surprisingly, no one has come this entire time.

Adam sits on my abdomen while everyone else is holding me down to the ground. I try wiggling harder, but none of my attempts have worked, and it's even harder now that Adam is sitting on me.

"Don't fret so hard. You won't remember any of this soon. One day you will be mine, but for now you must forget all this."

I feel the poke of the needle jabbing onto my left shoulder. My eyelids are feeling heavy ... and my body feels extremely drowsy. One thing leads to another, and I doze off.

§

I awaken to the sound of Elliot's footsteps approaching the bedroom. My entire back is drenched in sweat. What an absolute nightmare. Except it didn't feel like some typical horrendous dream but more like a forgotten memory.

I still feel the excruciating pain on the upper left side of my abdomen where Adam took the biopsy of my spleen. I'm afraid that he ruptured something inside of me, and there's nothing I can do about that. I don't see myself finding a new doctor to fix this problem once I escape, since this experience has been way too traumatizing.

"Hey, you OK? You've been talking in your sleep."

My breathing grows rapid. "I'm ... um ... I'm fine." I avoid eye contact. It's all coming back to me, but how is this possible? What did he put in that shot that made me forget?

Elliot leaves the room ... finally. I thought he'd never leave. I don't need his ungenuine comfort at such a time of distress.

For the past hour, I've been staring up at the ceiling, knowing that I won't be escaping anytime soon. I won't get far with dysfunctional legs, so I'm stuck here.

Elliot comes into the room holding a bowl of soup and a spoon.

"You hungry? I made you broccoli cheddar soup."

Even though having that soup sounds so nice right now, I'm not giving in to his bribe this easily. If this is how he plans on gaining my trust, it's not happening over soup. He probably thinks that I'll assume that he's doing this out of the kindness of his heart and forgive him. Not happening. Elliot is no better than Adam.

He brings the soup bowl closer to me, and I knock it to the ground. The bowl breaks into a gazillion pieces, and the spilled-soup mess is all over the floor.

"Are you freaking serious right now? Why would you do that?"

I sneer. "I know a bribe for my trust when I see one."

Elliot grows panicked as Adam steps get closer to the bedroom.

"What the hell is going on?" Adam yells. He stares at me with a stern expression on his face. "Is Violet misbehaving?"

Elliot stutters nervously. "No, um, I ... of course not. I'm the one who spilled the soup."

At first, I didn't think that Elliot would care to take the blame for me. Is this some sort of trick? Adam's hostile glare burns a hole in Elliot's face.

"Elliot, can I have a word with you?"

"Yeah. What's going on?"

Adam grits his teeth. "Outside."

"Oh, right. I'll clean this up after then."

Elliot steps out the bedroom with Adam, but I can still kind of pick up on their distant conversation.

"Why the hell are you defending her for not being docile?" Adam whispers.

"Come on, Adam. Give her a break. The girl has been through enough. Her being trapped here is enough of a punishment."

I hear a loud slap. I'm assuming that Adam struck Elliot.

"Now, don't make me believe you're starting to grow soft all of a sudden." I can hear the rage in Adam's distant voice.

Elliot stays silent.

"Plans have changed. Now, here's what I want you to do." Adam peeks through the door to check on me before continuing to talk to Elliot.

They both walk away further, and I can't hear a single word that's being spoken by them, but whatever Adam is planning for me has to be bad. Why else would he pull Elliot aside for something if it's not damaging to me? The real question is, Will Elliot go along with what Adam wants him to do, since he defended me earlier?

Elliot returns to the bedroom without Adam. He has rags and a broom in his hands. He starts cleaning up the mess.

"What did he say?" I ask skeptically.

Elliot avoids eye contact as he sweeps up the shattered bowl pieces.

"Um, well, he just told me the plan for tomorrow's physical."

My eyes tear up … again. "So … so, there really is another physical tomorrow, huh?"

"I'm afraid so."

"Elliot, you have to help me. Look, I know you're not like him. If anything, you seem a lot nicer than him."

Our eyes meet the moment he finishes sweeping and wiping the floor.

He exhales for a while. It stays silent for a few seconds longer. "How about you escape? I'll act as though I didn't know that you left."

I point to my legs.

"Ah, right." He rubs the back of his neck, "I can bring you back home?"

I sob through my words. "Yeah, Elliot, but it won't be long before Adam gets to me again."

Elliot lies down next to me and wraps his arms around my body. I don't stop him, because it feels really nice. We lie in silence for a while.

"So? Will I be receiving epidurals on a daily basis now?"

"I don't know."

Elliot sits me up and puts my shoes on.

"Wait what are you doing?" I panic.

I push Elliot's hands off me. "No. *No!* Elliot, No! I'm not doing the physical now! I'm not ready!" I cry.

Elliot shushes me, covering my mouth with his hand. "Shh. Don't make any noise. OK? We're going for a ride. Just trust me."

I pause my weeping and slowly nod, and Elliot removes his hand from my mouth. Is he helping me escape?

"You're not taking me home, are you?" I whisper.

"Shh. We'll talk in the car."

Elliot carries me down the stairs, and we walk past the back of the couch in the living room, which is where Adam is watching TV.

Once we get to the front door, Elliot's keys jingle as he picks them up from the small table near the exit.

"Where you going?" Adam raises his voice without turning around.

Good, Adam doesn't see me. Hopefully, he stays that way until we finally get outside.

"Um, I'll be back in a few. Just gotta pick up Dad's medication from the drug store," Elliot says as he turns the doorknob.

"What's Violet doing?" Adam asks.

"Oh, her? Yeah, she's sleeping. Let's not bother her."

Elliot finally leaves with me in his arms and puts me in the passenger seat of his car.

"OK, now, where are we going?" I ask impatiently.

"Remember that girl Nicole that Adam is friends with?"

I nod.

"Well let's just say, they aren't friends anymore, and she's going to be happy to see you."

I'm so confused right now. How in the world is Adam's ex friend going to help me?

"OK, and? What does this have to do with me?"

Elliot side eyes me and smiles. "You and Nicole are gonna have a little chat."

I raise my brows at him. "A chat?"

"I let her know that we are on our way to her house, so don't worry, we aren't showing up uninvited."

This all seems way too good to be true. When did he have time to call her?

"Just so you know, Elliot, the only reason I'm trusting you at all is because I don't have any other choice."

Elliot winks at me. "You're welcome."

Surprisingly, Nicole doesn't live so far. The ride is just under five minutes long.

Nicole steps outside her front door to welcome us in.

Elliot carries me out of his car, and Nicole has a puzzled look on her face.

"He gave her an epidural," Elliot tells her.

"Oh. I see," she answers. She doesn't seem the least bit surprised.

"All right, well, come right in."

"Thanks," I say.

We all sit on her couch, where Elliot sits me upright.

"Are you OK?" Nicole asks me.

"She's a bit shaken up from Adam's attentions," Elliot replies.

A bit? That's an understatement.

"Guys, why am I here?"

She puts her hand on my knee. "Because I'm sincerely sorry. I honestly had no idea about Adam's real intentions. I was just doing what I was hired for."

I freeze. "I'm gonna need a little more information than that. What do you mean you were hired?"

Before she responds, I notice that weird necklace around

her neck that looks like the one Elliot wore on our first date. Like a microphone. That's odd.

"I was hired to act as though I am one of his fangirling patients who ... well, you get the idea."

I roll my eyes, which seems to arouse surprise on Elliot's face.

I stare at the mike necklace around her neck.

"I like your necklace," I say quickly.

Nicole grabs onto it, and she looks suddenly alarmed.

"Oh, um, thanks, but yeah, I'm sorry I was just an actor. None of it was real."

Her words sink more deeply into my thoughts, and I can feel my face losing its color.

"Why admit this to me now, I wonder? And why aren't the other actors confessing this with you?"

Elliot and Nicole exchange glances. It's almost like they are hiding something from me. I should really be careful around Elliot. After all, he really can't be trusted.

"Well, um ... they still, um, work for him, but ever since me and Elliot talked more, I started to really feel bad for you, and I genuinely wanna help."

How pathetic. I'm not buying it, but I think playing along is a safer route to take.

I shrug. "OK. So, what do you suggest?"

"I know this is going to sound crazy, but I think you should marry him."

I stay silent so that she explains herself more. Nicole is a hell of a liar. She's still working for Adam, which is clear as day, but *marry him*? Is she out of her mind?

"If you show him just how desperate you are—that you are willing to marry him—then I guarantee he will be so turned off that he won't want you anymore. And I can help you."

I kind of wish I can laugh in her pathetic face. I mean, this is just ridiculous. If this is Adam's idea of convincing me to marry him, then he's out of luck. Really? Asking his paid actor is the best he could do? NOT. GONNA. HAPPEN.

"Mhm, great idea." I smile eagerly to give off the impression that I'll follow through with this when I have no intention of doing that.

Nicole raises her brows, clearly surprised. "Wait, seriously? You're not even gonna ask how I was hired?"

She clearly rehearsed more to say to me, so it must feel like a waste to learn her lines if I won't even bother questioning her further. The truth is, there's not much more I need to ask her. I'm just glad I caught her off guard. I'm still disgusted by her though. I wonder how much money she's making for this "work shift."

I attempt to move my legs and, thankfully, they seem to be moving again. The effects of the epidural must be wearing off. I got lucky this time, but the next time he does this to me, I won't be. I may not know much about medical stuff but I'm pretty sure that receiving an epidural on the legs can leave someone disabled permanently. I have to be clever for this escape to work effectively, or else this is basically my future.

"Yeah, I'll follow through with the marriage, but I think it will work best if you two let me go home. If I'm still in custody, then it won't be as believable. It's gonna seem like I'm saying anything just to be released."

Elliot and Nicole exchange glances, and Elliot nods at Nicole so lightly that it can easily go unnoticed. I'm guessing that Elliot gave her a confirmation signal.

"You're right. I agree with you, and remember, we're on *your* side."

"I'll drop you off home," Elliot says.

"No, no … no need. I can finally move my legs, so I'll walk home. I recognize this street, and I don't live too far."

"You sure?"

I smile and nod, standing up and making my way to the front door. My legs still feel weak, but at least I can walk even if it's taking some extra effort.

§

I left Nicole's house an hour ago, but I didn't go straight home. I can't bring myself to face my mom and face all the questions about a "sleepover" that never actually took place. I'm currently sitting on a bench at the park nearest to my house—since I can't walk too far with weak legs—and I'm about to call the guy I was supposed to go on a date with before Elliot drove me away to the medical office. The poor guy thinks that I ditched him, and I never got back to him about what actually happened. Once I tell him everything, it looks to me that I'll have found my own personal paid actor. Adam has an entire army, and here I am all alone fighting for myself. I need someone on my side, even if it means I have to pay for it.

14

Adam

I STARE AT ELLIOT WITH CROSSED ARMS, COMPLETELY disappointed. What an idiot.

"What do you mean you let her go? *Are you out of your mind?*"

"I know what you're thinking, but look at the bright side! She'll be back. I promise," Elliot says unconvincingly. He is rubbing the back of his neck and fidgeting uncontrollably, probably scared for his life—as he should be.

I don't say anything. I want this idiot to hear me loud and clear, but through actions, which speak louder than words. I strike Elliot across his face, and he freezes in place suppressing tears the way he usually reacts after I hit him.

"You know what I should've realized earlier?" I get up close to his face. "That if you want something done, you've gotta do it yourself."

Elliot sits down on the couch nearly crying.

"Look at yourself, Elliot. You can't even stand up to me. What makes your pathetic self think that Violet will want you after everything?"

"What are you talking about?" he stutters.

"I know the only reason you're helping me is to get closer to Violet, and clearly you're the last person she wants to see right now."

Elliot stands up abruptly, which somehow surprises me. Before I realize what he's going to do, he punches me in the gut. I bend over, coughing and suffering from the pressure build up on my stomach. I grab Elliot by the neck and squeeze as I watch him struggle to breathe. I release him slowly and let him speak.

"Not like she wants you either," he says as he catches his breath and coughs uncontrollably.

I stare into his fearful eyes, knowing damn well that he is aware that I won't have mercy if I end him on the spot. He hasn't been helpful enough to me. I grab him by his collar and lower my voice.

"Well, at least I didn't betray her. But you ..." I sneer, "You were her safe place, and now she hates you. Let that sink in."

I release his collar, dropping him on the couch. He sits there with his head in his hands. I can't feel bad for someone who planned to take what's mine. Elliot is two-faced, but I'm not. Violet should appreciate that about me, because I would never go behind her back. She needs me, and I have to save her. Healing and taking care of her for the rest of our years together was something I meant to do for my love. She doesn't understand that yet, but she will soon, once she realizes just how much she needs me. Violet won't be returning. I know that for sure, because I'm not the idiot who let her go so easily. I'm going to pay a visit to her house, assuming she can't hide away anywhere else. I'm taking her back, and this time I won't ever let her leave my sight again.

15

Violet

"WE'VE REHEARSED THE PLAN ENOUGH FOR NOW. DO YOU wanna relax?"

Andrew nods. I pour tea from the kettle and hand the teacup over to him.

"Wait ... how do you know that Adam will come looking for you?"

"Because, Andrew, it's clear as day that I won't be coming back to him, and he's not gonna take that lightly."

"Right. Well, he still hasn't shown up, and it's getting kinda late, so I should get going," he says suddenly.

My eyes travel to the old clock on the wall. It reads 10:05.

"Hold up. What if he shows up tonight? You won't be here to defend me."

Andrew hesitates. "Violet, this situation seems pretty serious. Why don't you call the police on this asshole? I mean, I'll defend you either way, but you can't just leave the situation alone like this."

I avert my eyes to the floor. I don't say anything in response, but I feel my cheeks beginning to heat up.

"Oh, hell no … you … you *like* this guy?" Andrew raises his voice, annoyed.

I don't answer. I'm not sure why, but I sort of want to cry. My eyes tear up.

"But how? You told me about all those horrible things he's put you through."

I exhale. "It's not that simple and I also have no proof against him," I finally say.

"Well, if you don't tell the police, then I will."

Before I get the chance to argue with Andrew, the doorbell rings. Andrew and I exchange fearful glances. I feel my heart sink to my stomach. We are in the kitchen, so my mom answers the door.

"Hi, can I help you?" my mom asks.

I peek behind the door with Andrew standing behind me, and I can't believe my eyes.

"It's him," I whisper.

"All right let's move." Andrew tries to push past me, but I push him back.

"Wait, no … are you crazy? Let's just be patient."

"I'm supposed to be defending you, not hiding from this smug jerk. So, I suggest that you at least let me try."

"Violet, hun, someone at the door wants to talk to you," my mom calls out.

"Here we go."

I come out hand in hand with Andrew, who is walking by my side. I feel safer knowing that I don't have to go through this alone.

My skin heats up the closer we approach Adam, but I remind myself that Andrew has got my back.

Adam crosses his arms. "Well, well, well. It seems to me that Violet has an unwanted guest on the premises."

Andrew grips my hand harder as he attempts to contain his anger. His rage is definitely contagious.

"I couldn't agree more. You don't seem desirable anyway." Andrew chuckles as he turns Adam's rudeness back onto himself.

One thing leads to another, and Adam pushes him back aggressively and grabs his collar. "Who the hell are you, punk?"

"Adam ... stop. Don't do this here!" I shout. I can't bear the idea of Adam beating Andrew, especially with my mom in the house. Thankfully, she heads upstairs, and I soon hear the water running, so she's probably taking a shower.

Adam pauses in his tracks and releases Andrew's collar. "Would you look at that? The coward herself can actually speak."

Adam's sharp stare cuts through me like a razor blade. " Leave her alone!" Andrew says, his voice cold and commanding as he blocks me with his body.

Adam sneers and chuckles manically. Damn it ... is he drunk? He seems more choleric than usual right now.

"Here's how things will play out. We'll either do this the easy way or the painful way," Adam says.

Andrew takes his phone out of his pocket and starts dialing. "Leave now, or I'm calling the cops!"

"The cops, huh? Good luck with that. My mom is a cop, so she'll have no trouble believing her own son's story over yours." He gets closer to my face. "And you," Adam grabs the back of my neck. "You're coming with me."

Andrew punches Adam in the jaw and presses the call button.

I gasp. "Andrew!"

"Stay back! I'm warning you," Andrew shouts at Adam.

Adam pushes Andrew's phone out of his hand and pulls a needle syringe out of his pocket.

"Give me back my phone!" Andrew yells.

The phone screen is broken, but the line connects with the 911 emergency dispatcher. For some reason, the call is muted, so the dispatcher can't hear us. I stare at the phone on the floor behind Adam's foot. My ears are starting to ring.

"911, what's the emergency?" the man on the line calls out.

Adam swiftly grabs my arm and holds the syringe needle a few centimeters away.

"Answer them and I jab her … I dare you!" Adam threatens.

My heart might just fly right out of my chest. The ground seems like it's jumping, and the room is spinning uncontrollably. The pain in my abdomen, where Adam did the biopsy, is worsening once again. It's intolerable.

Andrew looks more alarmed than a moment ago. He relaxes his furrowed brows and softens his voice, giving the appearance of calm, perhaps only now realizing just how crazy Adam really is. "Look … Adam, just calm down, man … take it easy." Andrew ends the call. "You see … I hung up. Just please put the needle away."

The tension in the room is elevating. I can't risk pulling my sweaty arm away now, or I'll get jabbed sooner than I can make a slight movement. My breathing becomes more rapid. I feel the poke of the needle penetrating my skin. Blackness takes over my eyes, and I feel my head meet the ground. Through the sound of my head throbbing, I can hear the sound of someone getting punched and a body dropping to the ground. The rest is hard to make out. My senses continue to blur as I doze off.

16

Violet

MY EYELIDS FEEL HEAVY, LIKE THEY ARE GLUED SHUT. AS I TRY
to open them, it feels as though they are still closed. The pitch
darkness overtakes the sight of my unfamiliar room. Wait,
no. It's not my room. It can't be. The last thing I remember is
collapsing to the ground when Adam jabbed me with a needle.
There's no telling if that was a dream, although I really hope it
was ... then I wouldn't have to worry about putting Andrew's
life in danger. After all, it's my fault that I dragged him into
this. It's a lot colder here than what I'm used to in my bedroom.
I'm definitely away from home. I feel as though the ground is
jumping or like I'm on a cruise. This could be a symptom of
dehydration. I don't remember eating anything yesterday or
even the last time I had a drink of water. I attempt to pull myself
up, but something is restricting my wrists. I don't know why it
took me so long to realize that I'm tied up. I'm not sure what's
holding my wrists together, since it is impossible to see in such
darkness. Wait a second. Where's Andrew?

"Hello! Anybody there?" I shout.

I hear someone cough out of sight, followed by a gasp. I'm not alone. Somebody must be nearby.

"Violet? Is that you?" a familiar voice speaks out.

There is hope yet. "Oh my ... Andrew? Thank God! What's going on? Where the hell are we?"

"I ... I don't know. Are you OK? Did he hurt you?"

My throat dries. I am in desperate need of water. Like, right now.

"I'm not sure. I can't see anything. I just feel kind of dizzy."

I hear grunting and shoes kicking against the floor.

"Crap! It's no use. I can't break out of these ropes. I need something sharp to cut through it."

Oh, so that must be what's around my wrists. It's too thick to even attempt any sort of escape.

"We have to get out of here before he gets back!"

"Back to where? We don't even know where we are."

I sigh. "Well ... not exactly. I sort of have an idea of where."

There's a pause. "What? Like ... you mean you've been here before?"

"I don't know, but if it's where I think we are, then I think I know where the nearest exit is. But we need a key, which I know only Adam has."

There's a good chance I'm back in the basement of the medical office. There aren't any windows, so it's impossible to tell whether it's day or night. How long had I been knocked out?

It's silent now.

"Andrew?"

"Yeah?"

"I'm sorry ... for all of this."

It's dead silent again. Is he mad at me? I mean, it's not my fault that we got abducted. I didn't intend for any of this to happen.

"You know, if you would've listened to me and told the police, none of this crap would have happened in the first place."

"I know but—"

"Stop!" he interrupts. "I don't want to hear it."

I don't say anything. I don't want to get him more heated than he already is. After all, he doesn't deserve to be going through this. This is my battle. Not his.

He softens his voice suddenly. "My brother is in the hospital."

"What?" That was so out of the blue.

"He's very unwell, and I promised I'd be back by morning to see him. He hasn't got much time left to live. If I don't make it out of here in time, that will mean I never get to say goodbye."

Oh. That's the last thing I expected him to say. I don't even know how to respond to this.

"I'm sorry. I didn't know ..." I sigh. "I wish there was something I could do to help. I should've never asked you to defend me."

"Then why didn't you take this hell to the police?"

The door opens abruptly, and a stream of light is visible through the crack for a few seconds. The door slams shut, and I hear the jingling keys turn in the doorknob.

The lights blink on and off as they get turned on by Adam. This must be a very old basement. Even the lights are weak and faint. I remember this dreadful place like it was just yesterday. I can't say that I miss the annoyingly strong scent of hand sanitizer. I was right. We're back, and I have a feeling escaping will be a lot harder than the last time.

Adam approaches me and sticks his hand into my pants and plants it on my thigh. I can feel the warmth from his hand on my cold skin.

I let out the loudest scream possible, and Adam slaps my shoulder and covers my mouth with his hand.

"Not a sound," he says sternly. "It's lunchtime."

So, it really is the next day, and I was passed out through the entire morning too.

My breathing comes heavy and rapid. It almost feels like I am hyperventilating. There's no telling what he'll do to me today.

Adam drags the food tray from behind him and raises the bowl. Whatever he's about to feed me must be nasty. It smells like hell in that bowl.

"I'm about to spoon feed you. If you don't comply, I will give you a shot. Understood?"

I nod desperately.

He scoops a spoonful of the green mush and holds it to my mouth.

"Open!" He commands.

I open my mouth slowly, and he shoves the spoon too far and it hits my uvula. Holy shit, BRUSSELS SPROUTS?

He knows I can't stand those. Ugh, great. I can't believe I told him that I hate brussels sprouts on our date. I never thought that he would use that against me.

I don't know what makes me want to puke more—the taste or the fact that he hit my uvula. I know he did that on purpose. He's obviously mad at me.

I gag uncontrollably, and Adam covers my mouth with his hand. Then he grabs the drink that's on the tray and forces me to chug the nasty, metal-tasting water.

"You're not throwing up on my watch. I can't afford for you to lose any weight."

He picks up another spoonful and holds it to my mouth.

I obey, opening it even though I'm trying not to throw up right now. I want to avoid getting the shot as much as possible. I squirm and make a face as I hold the green mush in my mouth, contemplating whether I should spit it out.

"Chew!" he orders.

Adam massages my cheeks with his fingers to aid in my chewing. I swallow the mush, but it feels like it's going to spew right back out of my esophagus. The next spoonful is waiting for my mouth to open. No. I can't do this anymore. I turn my face away.

"Open your mouth *now*!"

Tears sting my eyes and roll down my face. This is torture. "Please, Adam. Don't do this. I'm sorry for everything."

"Shut up! If you don't finish this entire bowl, I'll surgically insert a feeding tube into you. Then you'll really have no control over what goes into your stomach. Am I clear?"

"But ... but this makes me want to throw up," I stutter.

"If you behave, I'll feed you something more tolerable, but for now, you're being punished. Now, open your mouth before I do it for you."

What's most annoying is, if I throw up right now, he will get even more mad and jab me with the shot. I'm surprised that Andrew has been so quiet. Is he enjoying the fact that I'm getting tortured right now? After all, he is still really upset with me.

"Somebody, help!" I shout.

Adam covers my mouth again.

"Leave her alone, you asshole!" Andrew screams.

Oh, good. So, Andrew doesn't completely hate me.

Adam turns his head to Andrew. "What did you just say to me?"

"I said leave her alone, asshole."

I'm not sure what Andrew is trying to accomplish here, because he is the one who is tied up, and Adam has all the power. That's why I haven't been standing up to him. There's no way I can defend myself in this state.

Adam throws the bowl of green brussels sprout mush, aiming at Andrew's head. Thankfully, he misses. The floor around Andrew is spattered with shattered pieces of the broken bowl and green mush. I pity his nose for having to smell such garbage, but at least I won't have to finish eating that crap.

"One more peep from your mouth, and I will tase both of you while I prepare for Violet's surgery."

I shake my head at Andrew, signaling that he should keep his mouth shut. Otherwise, everybody gets hurt.

Andrew stays silent. I bet that was hard for him, but I'm glad he got the cue.

"That's what I thought," Adam says scornfully.

Adam looks back at me and gets close to my face. "Now. Where were we?"

Then, the unspeakable happens. Adam locks his lips to mine, and I taste metal. It's blood. Adam chews my lips till they bleed. I try to turn away, but he holds my face in place. The last thing I need is for Adam to suck face with me. The last time we kissed, it was actually very pleasant. This time feels like a punishment. That's probably because it is.

He rolls his tongue into my mouth, which makes me want to throw up even more. I feel like I am suffocating.

He finally releases me ten seconds later.

"For every time Andrew talks back to me, I kiss you as punishment. I promise it will be anything but pleasant."

At this point, I'd rather get jabbed with the shot than have him kiss me again. That was horrible. My lips are completely torn, and the thought of his saliva in my mouth isn't appealing anymore. I must have a strong stomach to have not thrown up so far.

Adam grabs my chin, raising it so I will look up at him

where he stands. "I'll be back to set up for your surgery. Don't do anything stupid."

He kisses my forehead and leaves into what looks like a walk-in closet. The door shuts. I am alone with Andrew.

I turn my head toward Andrew and see him holding a broken, sharp piece of the shattered bowl. Even though his wrists are tied together, he manages to cut the rope by arching his hand inward toward his wrists. Oh my God. He really does it. He cuts away the rope from his ankles using the sharp piece with his freed hands. He runs over to me and cuts through the rope around my wrists, which takes twenty cuts before my arms are free.

"Hurry. We don't have much time before he gets back," I whisper.

"I'm going as fast as I can," he whispers as he finishes cutting away the ropes from my ankles.

We both quietly run up the stairs to reach the locked exit.

"Crap!" I hiss.

"What?"

"The keys! Adam has them."

We walk back down the stairs and are confronted by Adam standing in front of us.

"I told you to not do anything stupid!" he yells. There's a vein pulsing in his neck. I've never seen him this mad.

Andrew ambushes Adam, grabs the keys from his belt, and throws them to me.

"Violet, *run!*" Andrew yells.

I pause for a second. Should I leave Andrew behind?

"What are you waiting for? Run now!" Andrew yells again.

I can tell that Adam is trying to get to me, but Andrew is fighting him back.

I run up to the exit and turn the lock with my sweaty,

shaking hands, and the keys drop down the stairs. Crap! I run back down the stairs, and as I grab the keys from the floor, I see Adam pulling out a shot from his pocket and jabbing Andrew, who collapses to the ground. I don't have time to worry about Andrew. I need to save myself.

I run up the stairs and open the lock before Adam gets the chance to catch up to me. I run through the empty medical office, bolting away through the exit to get outside.

I feel really bad for leaving Andrew behind, but what other choice did I have? If I would've stayed, that would probably have ended someone's life. I get goosebumps at the thought of that life being mine. I inhale, swallowing gallons of fresh air outside as I keep running as far as my legs can take me. The wind hitting against my ears makes it sound like I am in a helicopter. Suddenly, someone's hand covers my mouth tightly from behind me as they drag me into the back seat of their car. I can't see who abducted me again. Adam must have caught up to me. This is it … I lost everything.

I try to open the handle of the door, but it's not opening. I think the child lock has been turned on. A guy wearing a ski mask sits in the driver's seat and takes off immediately.

"Adam, I know you're mad, but this has gotten too out of hand." My voice trembles.

He drives right past the medical office and drives through a red light. Huh? I thought he was taking me back to the basement. I guess not.

"What are you doing? You're about to get a speeding ticket!" I scream.

I hope he does, because then the police will deal with him. Once we've gotten further away from the medical office, he takes off his ski mask.

"Elliot?"

Adam

I CAN'T RISK LEAVING ANDREW HERE ALONE WHILE I GO AFTER Violet. He'll wake up and definitely escape by then. I walk over to his still body lying on the ground.

"Get your ass up now!" I yell.

There's no response. I kick his thigh hard in hopes it will be enough to wake him up.

"Come on! On your feet!" I kick him again and again.

Panic overtakes me once I realize what I've done.

I tilt Andrew's neck back, yet his chest isn't moving up and down like it is supposed to. I put the stethoscope in my ears and the chest piece on his chest. There's no sign of a heartbeat.

He's dead ... I killed him.

No ... no. This can't be happening. I'm not a killer! It was an accident! I must have given him an overdose of tranquilizer through the shot. I can't call an ambulance now, not when it will be a matter of seconds before I find my wrists in handcuffs. As much as I prefer that Andrew is out of the picture, this is not what I meant. It would've been more satisfying knowing that he got hit by a car and got pronounced dead like that rather than found dead at my feet.

I drop to my knees and break into rage, screaming my lungs out. Tears stream down my face. My future ... it's gone. *Shit!* I was going to use this shot on Violet, but considering how oversaturated the dose is ... I could've killed her. My poor girl would've been dead thanks to me. What kind of doctor am I? It's OK. There's still time. Once I find Violet, I will take her back and perform the nasogastric intubation on her, which will be temporary, because the permanent feeding tube that I will surgically insert into her will go directly into her stomach. Then she will have no choice but to depend on me forever. She is *my* patient, and it's going to stay this way till the end of time.

I've called Elliot close to ten times, yet there's no answer. Where is this idiot? Wait a second. I can track his location. Ha! Of course, he would be stupid enough to leave it on. Unfortunately for him, I can use his stupidity against him. Considering the fact that we had a fight, he probably has Violet to get back at me. Although I am highly doubtful that she would leave with him, it would explain why his location is moving at a very fast pace. I'm going to order an Uber to follow Elliot, and once I find him, I'll make sure that he pays for what he's done. I don't want to have another dead body, but if it comes to that, I will do whatever I have to do. I'm ordering an Uber right now and it just occurred to me that there is no specific destination I can tell the driver to leave me at. I guess that leaves me with no choice but to take his vehicle. I order the Uber, and all that's left to do is wait. It says that he is a couple minutes away, which isn't so bad. It just occurred to me that I didn't get rid of Andrew's body, but once I get Violet back, I'll deal with his body after.

After patiently waiting for the longest five minutes of my life, the Uber pulls up, and it's a brown van, which absolutely disgusts me. First of all, I don't appreciate that I have to sit inside a shit-colored, moving piece of junk. It's the kind of brown that's as dull as dirt. It reminds me of Andrew's pathetic, shit-colored hair. My attention shifts to the driver, and luckily, it's a small, elderly guy. Oh my God, is this guy ninety? I think I can take him.

The driver rolls down the window.

"Hey, are you waiting for an Uber to pick you up?"

"Yeah, are you Gilbert?" I ask.

"Yep, that's me. Get in!"

If I'm going to steal this old punk's vehicle, I need him to get out first. "Hey, I'm having trouble walking. Can you give me a hand by helping me get into the car?" I limp and make it seem like I am about to fall to make him pity me.

"Of course, don't worry about it. I'll help you out."

His old, pathetic, short self finally leaves my ugly ride, and he approaches me with a big, toothy smile. Once he's close enough, I kick him in the crotch, and he bends over groaning. I push him down and stomp on his tiny head a few times, and he screams louder. Luckily, the area we are in is like a ghost town.

I quickly get behind the wheel, shift the gear to drive, and hit the gas. As I am speeding away, I check the rearview mirror, and I see the old guy is still on the ground struggling. What a weak ass. He's starting to get up, although now he's the one who's limping while trying to get to the car. Now that I have a vehicle, I check Elliot's location, and it's actually not too far away. It seems to have stopped near a gas station. My GPS says that I am just five minutes away. I follow the speed limit without exceeding it. I wouldn't want to get pulled over in this shit-colored stolen van.

18

Violet

"WHAT THE HELL IS WRONG WITH YOU! WHERE ARE YOU taking me?" I shout.

"Somewhere safe. Don't worry, we are a long way from Adam."

I crawl into the passenger's seat and put my seatbelt on. I'm not doubting that he is taking me from Adam, but that doesn't mean that I am openly trusting him either.

"And I should trust you because ..."

Elliot raises his voice. "You know, I'm sick of being Adam's pawn just like everybody else that's afraid of him, and I can't bear the idea of what he's putting you through."

Wow, they must have gotten into a fight. That could've been what made Elliot want to stop being Adam's minion.

"You seemed to be OK with it when Adam tortured me in the medical office."

Elliot isn't taking his eyes off the road for even a slight second. Clearly, he's got his priorities straight. I don't think this is just about me escaping Adam. This is about Elliot's escape too.

"I was never OK with it. If anything, he could have been worse to you if it wasn't for me being there to protect you. Did you really think I was there for Adam's benefit?"

I roll my eyes at him. "Yeah, it seemed like that."

"Well, all you need to know is that I was never in it for Adam. I just wanted to be there for you, and it would've been suspicious if I would have stopped him from his evil schemes and helped you. I mean, what did you expect me to do?"

He makes a fair point, but he could've gone about it differently.

"Um, obviously to defend me? To help me escape sooner? Why wait the very last minute to help me?"

He gets silent, but I don't need him to answer me, because I already know the answer. He's afraid of Adam, but so am I. It still doesn't explain why he didn't make a run for it earlier.

I sigh, "Elliot, why did you kidnap me?"

"I'm sure you wouldn't get in here willingly, since you clearly don't trust me," he replies, annoyed.

I look out my window. There are barely any cars on the road, and it looks like we are in a suburban area. Elliot drives into the nearest gas station, which is also empty.

"We're gonna get some gas really quick, because we have a long ride ahead of us."

My eyes bulge. Is he out of his mind? What does he mean by a long ride?

"Where are we going after getting gas?"

"I haven't thought that far ahead, but we'll figure it out along the way. This escape plan is kind of last minute."

"Why can't we just call the police on Adam?" I whine.

I know I'm overwhelming him with questions right now, but matters are really stressful.

"Violet, it's not that simple, because it's his word against mine. He will tell the police that I helped him, which gets me in trouble too."

I hate that he's right. So, what—now we just run away and hide like a bunch of helpless people? I wish I could punch something right now. This isn't fair, but I guess it's a good thing that I didn't tell the police earlier or Elliot would've been taken too. I have a feeling that won't be necessary, because he really is helping me.

I step out of the car with Elliot and slam the door. He's busy putting gas into the car, and I am fidgeting around impatiently. Wait a second … can Adam track Elliot? Crap! That should've been the first thing I asked him.

"Elliot?"

"What?" he impulsively screams.

I know we are both stressed out, but if we are being tracked, that doesn't make the situation any better.

"Can Adam track you?"

Elliot's eyes stick out, and he slightly opens his mouth.

"*Shit!* I forgot to turn off my location!" His hands are on his head.

"Oh my God, Elliot! I mean, seriously! You have got to be kidding me."

He pulls his phone from his pocket with his shaking hand and stares at it fearfully.

"What?" I ask worriedly.

My heart feels like it's about to jump out of my chest.

"It's Adam. He texted me that he found us."

Suddenly, a brown van pulls up into the gas station. That's weird, since it seems like nobody else comes here. Someone steps out of the vehicle—no, not just someone. Adam.

"Well, well, well. If it isn't the idiots who have forgotten to turn off their location." Adam is manically smiling and cackling like he is high on something. He looks very unwell, and his crazy eyes look extremely hungry for something. Or someone.

"Hurry, get in my car!" Elliot screams.

"I don't think so." Adam sprints after me and immediately has my neck in a choke hold as he pulls out a shot from his pocket.

He cackles maniacally as I try to escape his choke hold. "Nuh-uh. I wouldn't if I were you." He holds the needle closer to my skin, and I stare at it as sweat drips down my forehead. I don't miss the feeling of a needle penetrating my skin so aggressively. There's nothing I want more than to bolt away from Adam, but I'd sooner get jabbed than do anything else that's worse. This feels like déjà vu.

Elliot tries to move toward us to get me back but hesitates and flinches as Adam, who is probably grinning, is threatening me with the shot. I can't see Adam's face right now, but I can tell that he is completely choleric.

"Let her go, Adam. You're here for me, and I'll give myself up if you release her."

Why does he think that? I'm pretty sure that he's here for me, if anything. I'm the one who escaped his little medical prison down in the basement.

"Actually, I've come to collect." His voice is so histrionic and passive aggressive. "Get in!" Adam orders scornfully, leading me into his van while I am still in a chokehold.

I get into the backseat of the car as he holds me at needlepoint.

"If you get out of the car, I'll jab you. Understood?"

I nod, and he slams the door shut. I think he forgot to lock the car doors, since I can still run out, but I have to be sneaky about it when the time is right.

Adam pounces toward Elliot like an animal and kicks him

in the groin. Elliot bends over in pain and scrunches up his face. I can't even imagine how bad that has to hurt. Adam stomps Elliot down as he says something to him, but I can't really make out what he's saying from inside of the car. I quietly open the door to at least hear what's going on. I need to save Elliot. This is absurdly inhumane. Adam kicks Elliot's head as Elliot attempts to stand up. He falls back down to the ground. The next kick at Elliot's face causes a stream of fresh blood to come out of his nostril. Adam finally gives Elliot a chance to stand up, now that he has gotten Elliot weak enough to lose their fight.

"Come on! Let's see what you've got, you pathetic piece of crap!" Adam yells.

Elliot looks completely worn out from being stomped on so hard. Elliot throws a punch, which Adam swerves away from.

"Is that the best you've got?"

"Not even close!" Elliot screams. Elliot punches Adam in the face, which gets Adam even more hyper.

Adam kicks Elliot in the groin a second time. He shouts, "Violet doesn't belong to you! You really think she would choose you after you abandoned her?"

Elliot coughs up blood onto the concrete, and Adam continues kicking the life out of Elliot. Adam seems to enjoy this so much. What an absolute sadist.

I can't watch this anymore. Elliot is sacrificing himself for me, and I can't bear the idea of him getting beaten and kicked to death. I sneak out of the van and up close to Adam. Behind Adam is huge sheet metal that's wedged to the concrete ground. I kick Adam with all my strength in the back of his leg. Once he turns around, I kick him in the groin before he takes any further action. I can't even express the fear that has taken over my entire body, but I stand my ground.

"Violet!" Adam shouts. "You are being very disobedient, you bitch!"

He is about to pull out the shot from his pocket. but I kick him again, and he bends over in pain.

"You bitch! What have you done!"

Elliot tugs at his leg, and Adam falls to the ground where his head aggressively lands on the metal. Adam's eyes shut seconds later.

Meanwhile, I am so out of breath, and so is Elliot, who is coughing up blood on the ground.

I run up to Elliot and hug him.

"I'm so sorry." I weep.

Elliot lies his head down on the ground and closes his eyes.

"*No!* Elliot!" My tears drip onto his cheeks.

"Please, come back to me," I cry. "I do forgive you. You hear me? Just please, stay with me. I can't lose you now."

I lay my head on his chest, weeping my eyes out. This is all my fault. I should've gotten out of the van sooner. I dial 911 as fast as I can.

§

I've been in the waiting room of the hospital for a couple of hours now, and time is eating at me slowly. I tap my foot to the ground, fidgeting, as that's all that distracts me from my high levels of anxiety. Finally, the young, female doctor approaches me, and I sprint up toward her.

"Is he going to be OK?" I ask. My face still feels really sticky from earlier. It's probably from the sweat due to the craziness of the situation.

"Elliot is going to be fine, but his brother, Adam, is in a

coma. I'm afraid Adam's going to have to stay in the hospital under proper care and nourishment until he awakens again."

I smile at the thought of Adam being out of the picture. He may not be in jail or dead, but at least he is the least of my worries now.

"When can I see Elliot?" I ask impatiently.

"You are free to see him now, but he will be discharged later tonight once we have all of the papers filled out."

"Thank you, doctor."

"Also, how are you related to the brothers?" the doctor asks skeptically.

"Oh, Elliot is my boyfriend, and I'm not really close with Adam."

"OK, well, I was told that the detective wanted to see you regarding what happened to the brothers, so she will see you shortly."

My heart nearly skips a beat. A *detective*? This can't be good. Oh, that's right. I am about to be interrogated. After all, it is oddly suspicious why I would be there at the scene of the incident. I told the 911 dispatcher that the brothers got attacked by some mysterious guy wearing a ski mask, who arrived in a brown van. My story probably sucked and could've used some more support, but it was hard to think of something on the spot.

"Thank you for letting me know." I smile at the doctor.

She leads me to where Elliot's room is, and I thank her again. I don't bother going to check on Adam, since I want nothing to do with that crazy person.

He needs all the help he can get, and I'm glad he can't hurt me—or anyone—anymore. For now …

I knock on the opened door, and Elliot looks up at me.

"Can I come in?" I smile.

"Violet? You're OK!"

A tear escapes my eye, but I wipe it away. I sit beside Elliot's hospital bed and hold his hand.

"I am, but I'm more glad that you are."

He smiles warmly.

I exhale and look up. "Look, I'm sorry again for doubting you. I was just really scared that I'd be deceived again."

"Shh ... don't be. It's not your fault."

"Adam is in a coma," I blurt out. "I guess that means we're free." I laugh through my tears.

"Probably not for long though." Elliot shrugs.

"Yeah, I'm just concerned with the fact that the detective is going to be asking us questions." I fidget with my fingers.

He sits up in the hospital bed this time with a serious expression on his face.

"What? What do you mean? You're not gonna snitch on Adam, are you?"

"No, of course not! I'm not going to throw you under the bus like that."

Elliot sighs, relieved.

"OK, so what are you going to tell them?"

"The same as I did over the phone to 911. I told them that some guy in a ski mask pulled up in a brown van and attacked the both of you."

Elliot stares into space, lost in thought.

"So ... this could either completely end me or—"

"Look, Elliot, if you really think about it, Adam has no proof that you helped him, so if you snitch on him, I doubt that it will affect you."

Elliot seems unsure, but what other choice do we have? All the evidence will probably lead to Adam anyway, and it will look really bad if we lie.

"We can try, but that doesn't mean any good will come out

of this. It's not like the police can take a coma patient to jail, right?"

I smirk. "Or maybe he won't ever wake up."

Suddenly a woman who looks like she's in her early thirties steps into the room. Her hair is slicked back into a tight ponytail, and she is wearing a professional suit with a badge on her belt. Despite her youth, I find her very intimidating. Her eyes look as though they could see right through me.

"I was told that I will find Violet and Elliot here. I need to ask them some questions." Her voice is tough and insensitive.

"Yes, that's us. I'm assuming you're the detective," I say.

She holds out her hand and gives me a very firm handshake.

"I'm detective Mendoza, and I am going to ask you some questions."

I exchange glances with Elliot, who has a concerned look on his face.

"Um, OK. What are the questions?" I hesitate.

"Can you summarize what happened?"

"Detective, it was Adam. He abducted Violet, and we were escaping away to safety, but he caught up with us," Elliot blurts out.

The detective has plain, serious, lifeless eyes. She is really not messing around.

"Why didn't you go straight to the police?" she questions.

Elliot and I exchange glances again and get quiet for a moment.

"It didn't feel right to snitch on my brother. He is family. I couldn't do that to him."

I lightly nod at Elliot, reassuring him that he was smart to respond that way.

We end up telling the detective that Adam kept me tied up as a hostage in the basement of the medical office where he works. He was very disturbed, and he was into doing human experiments. My friend Andrew, who was also a hostage, helped me escape, but I don't know what happened to him. Elliot helped me get away, but once Adam caught up with us, he beat Elliot up. During the struggle, he tripped, fell, and hit his head.

"We received a report that the brown van was a stolen vehicle from an Uber driver. Charges will be pressed against Adam once he is awake. In the meantime, do you have the address of the office that he worked at?"

I nod. "Yeah, Elliot can provide you with that information."

The detective left shortly after, and I began to wonder what did actually happen to Andrew. After all, he did save me, and I owe him for that. I really hope that he's OK.

"See, Elliot? That wasn't so bad."

"Yeah, just wait till Adam wakes up." He shrugs.

We get quiet.

"Well, what now?" Elliot asks.

I lean in and kiss Elliot on the cheek.

"I'm so lucky to have you."

Epilogue

Violet

Two Years Later

I MIX SOME VEGETABLES INTO MY POT OF CHICKEN BROTH while listening to some great music blasting on high volume. Ava lightly bumps into my calf as she crawls around between my legs, giggling. She's trying to get away from Elliot, who's playing a catching game with her. Aww, look at those two go. I'm the luckiest mom in the world. I pick her up and hold her over my hip bone.

"My sweet pea, what are you doing?" I say in a soft, babying voice.

She plays peekaboo with me, covering her eyes with her tiny hands. I kiss her on the cheek as I dance around to the music and add some spices to my signature chicken soup.

"Elliot, I'm making your favorite for tonight!"

I feel Elliot hug me from behind and nibble at my neck, which tickles. I giggle and turn to face him.

"What's my hubby doing now?" I say playfully as I kiss him on the lips.

"Admiring his beautiful wifey," he responds, kissing me back.

I place Ava into her playpen, and Elliot swirls me around. We dance and fool around in the kitchen for a bit until our ankles feel sore. I fall onto the sofa and exhale. Elliot joins me, as we are so out of breath.

"We should do that again tomorrow."

"Without a doubt!" Elliot elbows me and smiles.

§

In the tranquil stillness of the hospital room, where the only sound is the steady hum of life-support machines, Adam lies motionless, trapped in an endless slumber for two years. Once a persistent pursuer, now a silent figure lost in the void of unconsciousness. A single fly disrupts the stillness as it lands upon his outstretched arm, triggering a subtle twitch. Suddenly, the monitors erupt in a frenzy of activity, and Adam's eyes flutter wide open.

About the Author

JULIANNA PINKHASOVA WAS BORN IN New York City and is a college student pursuing her psychology major. When she's not writing, she produces creative and comedic scripts for potential film sketches. Aside from her interest in film making, Julianna highly enjoys acting.

Printed in the United States
by Baker & Taylor Publisher Services